"You can't a
eyes—or an a
Dig

"That's good advice, but I have a feeling I can dig to China and I still won't find the truth."

"Well, you'd better find it," her father warned. "Your life depends on it."

He was right, of course, but suddenly the situation seemed overwhelming. She'd lost everything. The world felt upside down, with her father helping her and Grady kissing her. She couldn't think straight, much less creatively.

Behind the garage the dog barked once then quickly fell silent, as if remembering where he was. She spoke quietly. "What happens if I can't?"

"That's not an option. You're a Taylor and Taylors don't fail."

The connection Risa had felt between them shriveled. Her throat went tight as he stared sternly at her.

"Now, pull yourself together," he ordered.

Dear Reader,

The Partner is the first in a series of six related Superromance books. Set in Houston, Texas, the stories center on the deep and abiding friendship of the heroines, a relationship that springs from their shared experiences at the Houston Police Academy. When tragedy strikes in the life of my heroine, Risa Taylor, their rare sisterhood, so precious and valuable, is thrust into jeopardy.

I've heard it said that friends are the family we pick for ourselves. That is certainly the case with me. I have a lot of acquaintances, but there are only a few people I think of as true friends, and as such I hold them very dear. They're too hard to come by to be treated any other way.

As the perfect example, I'll tell you about one of my closest friends. She's a writer, too, and we met fifteen years ago through a writing organization. She was already published, but had stepped back from her career to care for her two babies. I was a wanna-be newbie. The common thread of reading and writing drew us together. Something deeper pulled us even closer. We see the world through a similar prism, and things that are important to me are also important to her. At the same time, we're different enough to keep ourselves entertained. We started talking at that long-ago meeting...and we haven't shut up since!

Losing any valued relationship is traumatic, but my heroine's experiences go beyond that. In one irreversible moment she loses her partner, her friends and her career. Then she meets Grady Wilson. He seems determined to deepen her losses, yet in the end he does just the opposite. He fills the holes in her life and helps her recover. In the hidden parts of her heart, however, Risa continues to miss her friends. Can the rift ever be repaired? Will the six women regain their closeness?

I'm sure you'll enjoy *The Partner* and the five stories that follow it, but in addition, I hope these books help us all realize the importance of our friends. Like the old saying goes, they double our joys and halve our sorrows. Treasure your relationships and work hard to keep them.

Kay David

The Partner
Kay David

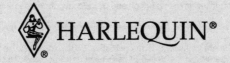

HARLEQUIN®

TORONTO • NEW YORK • LONDON
AMSTERDAM • PARIS • SYDNEY • HAMBURG
STOCKHOLM • ATHENS • TOKYO • MILAN • MADRID
PRAGUE • WARSAW • BUDAPEST • AUCKLAND

ISBN 0-373-71230-8

THE PARTNER

This one is for Leroy. He was a great partner and a loyal friend who will stay in our hearts forever.

Thanks go to Sherry, Anna, Linda, Roz and K.N. for allowing me to join them in this project. It was a pleasure to work with such a wonderful group of professionals.

CHAPTER ONE

"HAVE YOU BEEN DRINKING?" Risa Taylor glared at her partner, Luke Rowling, as they stood in the underground parking garage, the glow of a nearby light bathing them in orange.

They'd left headquarters only minutes before but Risa was already sweating, rivulets of moisture gathering between her shoulder blades and running down her back. August was not a good month for Houston and she'd started out the shift in a bad mood. She didn't need Luke out of it, too. She had enough to handle tonight.

When he didn't answer, she repeated her question. "I said, have you been drinking?"

"What're you gonna do if the answer's yes, Risa?" Leaning his elbows on the roof of their unmarked ride, a five-year-old Crown Victoria that had seen happier times, Luke gave her a lopsided grin. "Spank me for being a bad boy?"

She narrowed her eyes and stared at him.

When she'd joined the Sex Crimes Division at HPD, Risa had heard a lot of rumors about Luke

Rowling and his successes. According to some, his promotions had come too fast and too easily. Risa had been so thrilled to get her assignment in the prestigious unit that she hadn't cared, one way or the other.

Given that kind of success, though, she'd prepared herself for someone cocky and obnoxious, someone who'd be free with the constant teasing and sexual innuendo that were standard fare in the police department. She'd vowed ahead of time to dismiss any problems. Crap like that was part of working in a man's world, and you handled it and went on. But Luke had surprised her. Rumors aside, he hadn't come on to her even once, and more important, he'd turned out to be a much better cop than she'd ever expected.

Until lately.

Over the past few months, Risa had felt as if she were watching a car wreck in slow motion. The top-notch officer with the arrest record she'd envied had started to disappear, one piece at a time.

First, he'd come to work unprepared and confused, his clothing disheveled and his face unshaven. His hours had then become erratic and his behavior unpredictable. Last Friday, she'd thought she caught a whiff of alcohol when she brushed past him in the hall. This morning, when she smelled it again, she was sure.

"No, I'm not going to spank you." Slamming her car door, Risa walked around the rear of the vehicle and came to where he stood. Up close, the fumes were really strong and she wrinkled her nose in disgust.

"I'm not going to do anything with you, Rowling, including work. You're a disaster waiting to happen."

He put his hand on her shoulder and leaned closer. She had to hold her breath. "It's been a bad day, 'Isa. Gimme a break and I'll make it up to you, I promise."

She looked into his red eyes, the refusal she'd been about to voice dying on her lips along with her anger. The sudden and unexpected hopelessness in his gaze shocked her, but Risa hid it.

"What's up, Luke?" She spoke calmly, as if talking to an upset child. "What's wrong? You haven't been yourself for weeks."

He laughed, but the sound had a hollowness to it. "I haven't been myself?" he said. "What the hell is *myself*? Where am I? Who am I?" He was leaning so heavily on her that Risa had to brace her hip against the fender to maintain her balance. "Tell me how to be who I am, and I'll be happy to act like I'm supposed to."

The sound of voices echoed over the concrete and Risa looked up to see a group of uniformed officers spilling out of the elevator. She could feel their stares across the hot, steamy garage, and she tried to back away, but Luke held her fast. Someone snickered then laughter rang out.

"Tell me who I am, Risa." His pleading voice held a quality she hadn't heard before. "Tell me who I am 'cause I'm balancing on a thin line here, baby."

Risa lifted his hands off her shoulders and dropped them, his rambling discourse too strange to understand. "Go home and sober up, Luke. I'll call everyone and cancel tonight." She started to walk away, but his answer stopped her.

"I can't."

She turned and looked at him, raising an eyebrow. He shook his head slowly.

"You can't what?" she asked.

"I can't go home. Melinda says I'm a loser and a freak and she threw me out. I had to leave...." Looking as if he wanted to cry, he managed to choke back his tears at the very last moment.

"God, Luke..." Risa returned to where he stood, a wave of remorse for her callous attitude sweeping over her. "Shit, man, I'm really sorry."

And she was. Risa knew all about families shattered by the stresses their job generated—she'd grown up in one.

Luke lifted his gaze and their eyes met again. He seldom mentioned his wife, but Risa had suspected trouble at home for that very reason. They had one child, a little boy named Jason. Most happily married men she knew never shut up about their wives and kids.

"I'm very sorry," she repeated. "I had no idea things were that bad."

He blinked. "I didn't, either."

They stood in silence beside the car, Luke in obvious misery, Risa imagining the rumors that were sure to come. As soon as they'd become partners, a betting pool had started to predict when they'd hook up. The whole thing had irritated her—especially when she'd found out Luke wasn't bothering to deny the gossip—but over time, she'd been so grateful that he never hit on her she'd let it go. Apparently all he'd wanted were the bragging rights, so who cared? Now she couldn't help but feel sorry for him. She sighed heavily.

"Give me the keys." Holding out her hand, she gestured. "I'll drive, and you can sleep in the car while I talk to Sun."

His expression filled with gratitude, and he started to speak, but she held up her hand and stopped him. "Don't say anything," she demanded gruffly. "Just get a grip, okay? I can't do my job and yours, too."

He nodded and mumbled a thank-you, turning over the keys. A second later, she was behind the wheel and he was slumped over in the passenger seat.

Before she could wind the big car down the ramp and out to Travis Street, he was asleep.

She shook her head sadly. Risa had always wanted to be a cop, but the thing she hated most about the life was the way law-enforcement families suffered. Her mother had fled her cop-father before Risa had been out of diapers. The youngest in her family, and the only girl, she had three older brothers. They were all in the business, too, and between them, they had four ex-wives and one pending.

Luke's fate was sealed. He and Melinda would divorce, the kid would get hauled like a sack of potatoes from one house to another, then they'd each find someone else and start over, making a new spouse as miserable as the previous one. Risa flinched at her cynicism, but the truth couldn't be denied.

There was nothing she could do to change the situation, either. She turned her concentration to the job—where it belonged—and headed out, vowing, as she did every time she heard this story, that she'd never, ever end up with a cop herself.

She merged onto the Southwest Freeway, quickly hitting seventy. Traffic was light for a change, but then again, it was almost two in the morning. They'd wasted time talking down in the garage. Risa frowned. She hated to be late even though the woman she was meeting probably didn't care, unless she was charging by the hour, instead of the act. The guys made fun of Risa's obsession with time, but she didn't give a damn. They didn't make fun of her collars and she was getting close to topping every one of them.

If things went as planned tonight, Risa would be adding to that record, too. In the past six months, three hookers had turned up at Ben Taub Hospital with their faces pounded into bloody masks. Risa wanted the SOB behind the beatings so badly that she dreamed about making the arrest. After days of negotiating, she'd finally gotten one of the street hookers to agree to meet her and Luke. Sun, the friend of a friend of a friend of one of the girls who'd been injured, had sounded like a flake but who knew? Her information might help Risa find the slimeball.

Within minutes, Risa reached the part of Richmond Street known locally as "the Strip." For several miles on either side, bars stood next to massage parlors, which stood next to strip joints, which stood next to bars. The cycle seemed to go on forever, the signs the only thing that changed as one place went out of business and another one opened. The people who haunted the area stayed the same and so did the level of trouble they generated. When the clubs closed and the heat got to everyone, they'd take to the streets and drag race. Any sane person stayed away after eleven o'clock at night.

Slowing the Crown Victoria, Risa eased into the right-hand lane to join the line of vehicles waiting to get into the parking lot of Tequila Jack's. Luke was now snoring with his mouth open, his head propped up against the window.

A space of two—maybe three—feet opened up between her bumper and the car ahead of her, and immediately the Impala behind Risa honked. She glanced into her rearview mirror. A wildly colored low-rider was sitting on her tail, the two pachucos inside laughing and passing a bottle of something between them. She closed the gap then looked back again. Catching her glare, the driver raised his bottle in her direction as if to offer her a drink, then he made a kissing motion with his lips. She held his eyes until he looked away.

Fifteen minutes later she parked the Crown Vic, grabbed her bag and opened the car door. The air hit her like a soggy blanket, steamy and thick. She instantly broke into a sweat that dried into clamminess when she entered the air-conditioned club.

She felt eyes following her as she headed for the bar, but she was accustomed to the sensation. All her life men had watched her enter a room. In the past, they'd done so because of how she looked; they did it now because of how she acted. Obviously they didn't know who she was or what she did, but they knew she was someone they probably wanted to avoid. She'd worked on the attitude since she'd been a rookie and she had it down pat.

Pushing through the crowd, she took one of the empty seats at the end of a long Formica counter, the music so loud she could hardly think, much less hear. Screaming her order for iced tea, she ignored the bartender's arch expression. Lots of cops drank on the job, but not Risa. She did things by the book. A minute later, the aproned man came back with a glass of something amber-colored, a few listless ice cubes floating on top. The watery concoction tasted like used dishwater, but the glass was half-empty when she put it back down. In the meantime, the bar stool next to her had filled. She glanced to her right.

The girl who'd sat down didn't look old enough to even be in the place legally, much less be a hooker named Sun.

"You'll have to find another spot." Risa turned back to her drink. "I'm saving that for a friend."

"I *am* your friend." The teen's voice was high and sweet with a Hispanic lilt. Risa barely caught her words over the music and the girl had to lean in closer and repeat them. A tidal wave of cheap perfume came with her as she laid her fingers on Risa's arm. Her nails were painted with silvery polish. "It's cool…"

Risa looked down at the girl's fingers. They felt bony and slight as Risa lifted them and placed them back on the bar. "I really am waiting for someone else," she said firmly. "Why don't you—"

"You're waiting for me." She met Risa's eyes. "You're Risa, right? I'm Sun."

The image of the last beaten prostitute, Janie Seguaro, superimposed itself on the girl's childlike features and Risa had to take a deep breath. She shouldn't have been surprised, but she was.

"You're kinda young to hang out with Janie's crowd, aren't you?"

The teenager shrugged. "I guess. I dunno…" Reaching over, she took a deep pull from Risa's drink then made a face and stared at the glass. "Yuck! What *is* that—"

"It's iced tea—" A ripple of noise and then movement caught Risa's attention and she swiveled her bar stool to get a better look. As she did so, one of the two men who'd been in the car behind the Crown Vic—the driver, she thought—charged past, glancing at her for a millisecond before he kept going.

She wanted to ignore whatever trouble was taking place, but Risa was a cop through and through. Something inside her wouldn't let her stay where she was.

"Don't leave," she hollered to the girl above the noise. "I'll be right back."

Shaking her head, the girl frowned, her warning almost childlike in its naivete. "I wouldn't mess with that guy if I was you—he looks crazy."

"I'm used to crazy." Waving off the teenager's words, Risa pushed away from the bar and followed the pachuco. They were on the other side of the club when he came to a halt in front of a couple on the dance floor. Tightly twined around each other, the couple saw him a moment too late. The driver grabbed the second man, ripped him away from the woman and threw him to the parquet, screaming in Spanish as he did so.

Risa felt her pulse rate increase. She'd been off patrol for almost three years, and she hadn't had to deal with this kind of stupidity in ages. She glanced around for the bouncer but he was nowhere in sight. Pulling out her cell phone, she speed-dialed Luke and prayed he wasn't too far gone to wake up.

"Get in here," she yelled above the music. "I've two drunks going at each other and I need some backup!"

Flipping the phone shut without waiting for his answer, she pulled back her jacket to show her shield and gun, then yelled, "Police," striding to the men who were now tussling on the floor.

"Okay, that's it, ladies," she barked. "The cops are here. Stop right now and let's all cool down."

They paused long enough to look up at her then

they resumed their drunken, ineffectual swings, missing their mark more often than not. Bending over with a curse, Risa jerked the nearest one to his feet and twisted his arm behind him. That's when she realized the one on the floor was the second guy from the car. They'd come together to the club and now they were fighting. She rolled her eyes, then kicked at the boot of the one who was still down. "I'm Officer Taylor, HPD. Get up," she commanded. "We're taking this outside."

To her surprise—and relief—he staggered upright. Yelling at the crowd to disperse, she pushed both men ahead of her. When they reached the door and tumbled outside, Risa wasn't sure which was sweeter—the comparative silence of the nearby traffic or the muggy air she'd cussed before. After the bar, both offered a cleansing change.

Immediately the men went at each other again, wrestling and rolling around the steaming pavement like a couple of schoolboys, finally disappearing behind a nearby parked car. Risa considered leaving them to beat each other silly, then she changed her mind. She'd make Luke handle them. She yanked out her phone and dialed again. "Get over here, Luke!" she said angrily. "I need some help, dammit!"

He muttered something that sounded like assent and she hung up the phone, turning back to the two drunks.

One of them was gone.

The other one, now standing, held a gun.

Pointed straight at her.

Risa's breath caught in her chest and she froze, her mind spinning. A thousand thoughts came and went in the space of a single second, but only one stood out: she held the highest rating the shooting range awarded but there was no way she would get to her .44 before he could fire. For the moment, she was stuck. She licked her lips and held up her hands, palms out.

"Look, buddy, this isn't the time to do something stupid, okay? Drop the weapon and kick it away. My partner's on his way." Just to be sure, she repeated herself in Spanish. Her accent wasn't perfect, but the message was clear.

He said something she didn't catch, this time in English, then from the corner of her eye, Risa saw the other man rise from the pavement and start forward. She cursed under her breath—she thought he'd run off. Edging to her left, she stepped closer to the nearest car and away from the club's door. She didn't need any civilians getting popped, too. The one with the gun kept her in his sight, moving with her and spewing another rapid-fire burst of Spanish. She caught only bits and pieces, but it was enough to make her realize he wasn't drunk. He was stone-cold sober and his hand was steady.

"Put the gun down," she said evenly. "We don't have to make this any harder that it already is."

His face was slick in the neon light of the bar's sign. He said nothing.

"I've called for backup," she warned. "There's going to be a hundred cops here any second and they're not as patient as I am. They're men. They like to shoot."

His eyes widened, but he still didn't answer. By this time, they'd almost traded places. She wondered for a second why he'd let her manipulate him, then she realized he'd wanted to get where he was—the car she'd been standing by was the low-rider.

Later that night, and for weeks afterward, Risa replayed the scene over and over inside her head. There had to have been something else she could have done, she agonized, some other path to take, but at the time her choice seemed like the only one.

Speaking in Spanish once more, the driver jerked his head at his friend, who suddenly appeared by his elbow. He now had a weapon, as well, Risa realized with growing panic.

As she debated her chances of trying to fire regardless, the men exchanged a glance, and that split second was all she needed. Ripping her weapon from the holster beneath her arm, she aimed and screamed. "Drop your guns! Drop them now!"

A second later, Luke rounded the corner.

The men hesitated, then they pivoted in unison toward Luke, shooting blindly as they turned.

CHAPTER TWO

RISA SHOT BACK.

When she stopped, three men lay on the sidewalk.

Down the street, sirens filled the silence, their wails growing louder as the police cars neared. With the part of her brain that wasn't operating on automatic, Risa realized Luke had to have called for backup before he'd gotten out of the car.

The door of the club flew open and she swung her weapon toward it. Whoever was behind the door thought better of their actions and it instantly shut again, slamming against the frame so hard a piece of wood popped off.

The taste of fear filling her mouth, Risa approached the men with her gun extended. They weren't moving, but Risa was a woman who didn't take chances. She kicked their weapons under a nearby car, then bent down to the first man. He was slumped against the edge of the building and he sat in a spreading pool of blood.

He was dead.

The second one had a pulse but it was thready.

She reached Luke's side, her pistol still pointed at the other two as she dropped to her knees on the dirty pavement. Pressing a finger against his neck, she searched for a rhythm. Her own heart was beating so fast all she could feel was the rush of blood inside her veins. She took a deep breath then held it, pushing her finger deeper into the side of his throat.

His eyelids fluttered open and she nearly passed out with relief.

"Hang on," she said breathlessly. "Help's coming, Luke. Hang on, okay?"

He smiled sweetly and said, "Okay." Then his eyes rolled back and he went completely still.

GRADY WILSON HATED when the phone woke him up at four in the morning. The news was never good, he thought, fumbling for his glasses with one hand and for the lamp with his other. No one called that early in the morning to tell you you'd won a trip to Tahiti or that something had come up and your in-laws were not going to visit after all. Life didn't work that way.

He picked up the receiver and answered. "Wilson here."

"We've got trouble." Stan Richards, Grady's boss, sounded somewhat more awake than Grady but just barely.

"Imagine that." Grady tested his theory. "I thought you might be calling to give me a raise."

"You don't need a raise," Stan said sourly. "You've already got more money than God and you're probably going to quit next week anyway."

Grady ignored the money comment—he taught two night courses at the University of Houston on the side, so everyone thought he was rich. They had no idea college professors were as badly paid as cops. "You might be right about the quitting part," he said instead. "I'll decide after I hear about this trouble."

Richards's voice became serious. "It's bad. In fact, it doesn't get much worse. We've got an officer down over on the Strip."

"Dead?"

"Not yet, but it doesn't look good."

"Damn." Grady swung his legs to the side of the bed. "Who was it? Anyone we know?"

"Guy by the name of Luke Rowling. SCD."

"Sex Crimes? What'd he do? Wander into a bust or something?"

"We don't know right now. Chief Tanner got called so I got called so you got called. Go find out. I'm supposed to report directly to her personal assistant."

"Directly?"

"Did I stutter?"

"Well, no, but—"

"The guy's partner is Risa Taylor. You do know her, don't you?"

"'The Body' Taylor?"

"The one and only. You're a lucky man."

Grady moaned. "I'm too damn old for this, Stan. Call someone else—"

"Can't do that. It's certainly not official but rumor has it, you were requested for the case. Taylor's family is true blue and she's tight with the chief. I suspect the Iron Lady wants this done right with no questions left."

"So? What's that got to do with me?"

"I don't approve of your techniques, but you *are* the best. When you're finished with it, everyone will know the case is tighter than a gnat's ass and they'll be satisfied." Grady heard papers shuffling, then Stan spoke again. "They're still on scene, Fifty-six eighty-nine Richmond, Tequila Jack's. Samuel Andrews is the homicide lieutenant."

As Stan hung up on him, Grady realized what was going on. Chief Tanner might have requested Richards to report directly to her assistant, but she wouldn't have asked for Grady. Stan had put him on the case because he didn't like Grady and had probably wanted to call him out at this ungodly hour.

A former instructor at the Police Academy, Catherine Tanner had been the HPD commander for some time, but Grady's direct interactions with the woman had been too limited for her to ask for him, even if she were inclined to do so. Despite the gossip he'd heard about her, she was supposed to be fair and levelheaded, but a few people thought she'd gotten her job through connections rather than talent, and rumors continued to circulate about some type of vague corruption going on at the higher levels. Fair or biased, crooked or straight, it didn't matter to Grady. He only delivered the truth.

Fifteen minutes later he was dressed and in his car. Fifteen minutes after that he pulled into the parking lot of the bar. Grady had the feeling he could have found the place without the yellow-and-purple neon sign of a fat man wearing a huge hat and holding a margarita glass. Dozens of cop cars with flashing red lights were parked haphazardly on the sidewalk and in the street. Nearly that many television vans lined the street on the opposite side.

Pushing through the reporters and hangers-on, Grady spotted Samuel Andrews. Simultaneously yelling into a cell phone, talking to two other cops and answering a reporter's questions, the African-American lieutenant saw Grady and motioned him forward.

Grady nodded but took his time, looking around first. A blue plastic sheet covered a body, but it was the only one. Scanning the scene, he searched for Risa Taylor. He'd popped off about her nickname, but in truth, he wasn't sure he'd even recognize the woman. She was supposed to be a looker and very, very smart…so naturally most of the male cops hated her and/or lusted after her. Grady couldn't think of a more volatile mix inside a police department—resentment *and* sexual tension. Yipperdoodle, he thought dryly. This was going to be a real fun case.

He came to Andrews's side and waited for his turn. Andrews handled everyone else smoothly and quickly then he faced Grady, his expression wary, his demeanor less friendly. Grady barely noticed. He was accustomed to the low-level hostility that followed him wherever he went. Everyone hated Internal Affairs.

They shook hands. "Bad night," Grady said. "Any news on the officer who was shot?"

"I wouldn't be counting on him for the next shift. They took him to Ben Taub but he looked like he was already gone."

Grady held back a flinch. Most of the patients who were sent to the trauma hospital were so bad the docs swore they brought the dead back to life more often than they healed the sick.

"Where's the partner?"

"EMS guys took her, too."

"She was hurt?" Grady's voice held surprise. Stan had said nothing about this.

Andrews lifted his hand and drew a line down his cheek. "Just a graze. Didn't look too bad but you know the medics. She tried to stay then finally gave in." He tilted his head toward the blue-covered mound behind them. "That's Juan Doe, *número uno* over there. *Número dos* went to Taub with the rest of the party, but I think he's had his last enchilada.''

Andrews continued his explanation and Grady listened, his eyes going to the other side of the parking lot, where support guys had begun to crawl between the cars and underneath the bushes. Every once in a while, they'd stop, open a baggie and drop something inside.

''Any questions?'' Andrews finished.

''Not for now.'' Grady always let the lieutenants talk, but he got his real information from the officers and the scene itself. ''I'll be in touch, though.''

Andrews nodded with a dour expression. ''I'm sure you will.''

Grady wandered for another half hour, talking to the uniforms and letting the details register. He was just about to leave for the hospital when he overheard two of the techs. They'd been crisscrossing the parking lot, looking at the cars and trees.

''Even I coulda hit something,'' one of them said, shaking his head. ''That many shots fired? These guys musta been blind.''

Grady stopped. He knew a lot of the crime-scene technicians, and for the most part, they were friendlier to him than the officers. ''What's up?''

They looked up and greeted him. ''No slugs,'' the nearest one explained. ''I don't know what these guys were smoking, but they musta been shooting into the sky." He held up his baggies. "Plenty of shells, but no slugs yet."

"Keep looking, gentlemen. I'm sure you'll do your best for the glory of HPD."

They grinned and returned to their search as Grady headed for his car. The techs always said they couldn't find the slugs, but sooner or later they located them. Lodged in telephone poles or buildings, tires or pavement, the spent bullets hid themselves well. Once, the day after a shooting, they'd had a guy bring a motorcycle into the station. Without even realizing it, he'd driven by a holdup in progress and caught a slug in his tire. When he'd heard the news that night, he figured out why he'd gotten a flat.

Back on the Southwest Freeway, Grady headed for the medical center.

AGAINST THE WISHES of her father and her three brothers, who followed him in everything, Risa had attended the Houston Police Academy at twenty-one, the first year she'd become eligible. The rivalry, or maybe it was animosity, between her and her siblings was nothing new—they would have disapproved of anything she did short of becoming a nun—but her father's reaction had stung. Somehow, deep down, Risa had always thought that if she followed in his footsteps he might finally give her the same kind of attention he'd lavished on her brothers.

She'd been wrong.

When she'd told him she'd been accepted, Ed Taylor had frowned and muttered something about regret, then he'd disappeared into the garage of his aging home in Meyerland where Risa had grown up. She'd started after him, then she'd spit out, "What the hell," and had left, understanding, better than ever, how her mother must have felt when she left him. If you didn't see the world the same way Ed Taylor saw it, you were worthless to him. No wonder her mother had hit the road and never looked back. Risa got a Christmas card from her yearly and that was it. The lack of communication had hurt until she'd finally understood.

After she began her classes, the ache eased even more. Time had something to do with it, but more significantly, she made friends. She'd never been very good at that—and she still wasn't—but the five women she'd met during the six-month course were different from any she'd ever known.

Except for one, they surrounded her now, their faces etched with concern as she sat on the table in the emergency-room cubicle. Hearing the officer-down call and recognizing Risa's partner's name, they'd come in from every side of town. Risa was incredibly grateful for their company and support. If she'd been the kind of woman who let herself say so, she would have broken down and told them what they meant to her.

Abby Carlton stood the closest, her hand warm on

Risa's back as she patted her shoulder in a comforting way. At twenty-nine, she was nearest in age to Risa's twenty-seven, but she was the "mother" of the group. In a heartrending decision, she'd dropped out of the Academy to follow the love of her life, but things hadn't worked out. She'd returned to Houston a year later to complete her classes, ending up in patrol and doing extra duty on the Crisis Intervention Team. Her warm eyes were filled with sympathy and pain, not just for Risa's injury, which was minor, but for everything that had happened in the past few hours.

Crista Santiago stood on the other side, fiercely gripping Risa's left hand. A Latina from the east side, Crista was thirty-three. She'd had a difficult time growing up in Houston's barrios, but she'd risen above her former life and come out a survivor. A detective, she was tough…and gorgeous. She swung her dark hair away from her face as she leaned closer.

"Everything will be okay, *chica*." As if her words could make it so, Crista spoke with confidence. The only hint she was upset was the Spanish that slipped out apparently before she could stop it. "Thank God, you got the sorry *cabrones* who did this…"

Risa squeezed Crista's hand in acknowledgment then dropped it as Lucy Montalvo spoke from the foot of the gurney. "You got them both?"

Lucy was in the Missing Persons Unit of the Investigations Command. She was single-minded and ambitious and she'd made her way up the department just like Risa had—by working hard and being determined. Neither of them had a lot of free time to do things together, but out of all the women, Risa felt closest to Lucy. For good or for bad, they each valued their careers more than anything else in their lives.

Risa nodded.

"That's some kind of shootin'. Those hours at the range finally paid off."

"I didn't have a choice," she answered quietly. "When Luke came around the corner, they opened up."

"You did what you had to, Risa." Mei Lu Ling spoke from the other side of the room. Leaning against the wall, her thin form dressed in black, she looked every inch the successful businesswoman she'd once been. She was a valuable member of the White-collar Crimes Unit, putting that experience to good use. She'd be a lieutenant by this time next year, Risa guessed. Even-tempered and measured in her ways, Mei Lu offered sound advice now. "Don't look back. You did what you had to."

"I know," Risa lied. "But it all happened so fast and then boom! It was over, just like that. Luke was bleeding and I told him to hang on and he said he would, then…" She looked down at her hands. They should have been shaking, because she was on the inside, but they lay in her lap, perfectly still with streaks of dried blood on them. She raised her eyes. "Then he died anyway. He was gone before the ambulance even got here."

Silence filled the cubicle as Risa's words seemed to hang in the air.

"Have you heard from Catherine?" Crista asked after a moment.

Risa shook her head. Catherine Tanner's presence would have made the group complete, but she would be swamped right now with other duties. She'd been one of their instructors at the Academy and now at forty-five she was the oldest and most experienced of them. She was also the chief of police. Only one other woman in Houston's history had served in that position and she'd been appointed by a female mayor. To the majority of the force that had meant she didn't count.

"She won't come," Lucy said, echoing Risa's thoughts. "She can't appear to be too close to Risa right now or people might read it wrong. Plus she's got to deal with the media and IA and everything else—"

"Including Luke's family." Abby turned to Risa, her expression anxious. "He was married, wasn't he, Risa? Did he have any children?"

Risa nodded slowly, instantly deciding the details of Luke's disintegrating home situation would be a secret she would keep. "His wife's name is Melinda, and yes, they have a little boy," she answered. "I think he's three, maybe four..." Her sentence petered out as her chest tightened. She hoped the poor kid would get a better deal than she had, but any way you sliced it, growing up in a one-parent household was not for sissies.

The curtains surrounding the cubicle parted and the doctor who'd stitched Risa's cheek stepped in, a male nurse by his side. Pulling a piece of paper from his pocket, the physician handed it to Risa while the other man began to clean up the remnants of bandages and tape scattered over the counter.

"That's a script for a painkiller," the doctor said. Retrieving another one from his other pocket, he held it out, too. "And this is for some sleeping pills. You might have some trouble the next few days—"

Still woozy from the shot he'd given her to stitch her face, Risa shook her head...a little too hard. She gripped the table. "I don't need it."

"You've just been through a very traumatic situation. Are you sure?"

She stood up and the room spun. "I'm very sure," she answered. "I don't take stuff like that."

His wavering image split into three men in three white coats. Each of them nodded. "All right," he said with a sigh. The sound said he'd dealt with cops before. They were all macho—the men *and* the women.

Risa nodded—a big mistake—then she walked out

of the cubicle, her friends on either side supporting her in more ways than one.

THE WAITING ROOM WAS a blue sea and it would remain so until Luke's body was released. That's the way it had always been done when an officer got shot and Risa expected the tradition would never change. She entered, then stutter-stepped slightly, Abby clutching her right elbow, Lucy still holding her left. Their grips were firm but discreet. Any sign of weakness from a female cop, even one who'd just been shot, set them all back.

"Hang tough," Crista murmured from behind her. "We'll talk to the widow then get you out, okay?"

Risa nodded, the word *widow* throwing her for a second.

The women waded en masse through the uniforms, eyes watching from every corner of the room. In truth, the majority of the men they worked alongside were okay, but the few who weren't pleasant were a vocal minority. Risa heard someone mutter, "...better partner this wouldn't have happened..." then she found herself staring at David Kinner. A fellow S.C.D. officer, Kinner was rude, repulsive and tried his best to make every woman on the force feel unwanted. Risa read his lips as he leaned toward the cop on his right and spoke.

"Five butts, one brain..."

They'd almost come to blows the first time he'd

uttered the insult. She and her friends, still in the Academy, had been passing his table in the cafeteria when he'd said the words just loud enough for them to hear. Risa had immediately questioned his manhood and his alleged affinity for farm animals, but her comeback hadn't been enough to quiet him. He was persistent as well as stupid.

She ignored Kinner's remark and stepped before the thin, pale woman who'd been married to Luke.

Melinda Rowling was in her late twenties, maybe early thirties at the most, but grief had done its job and at the moment she could have easily passed for forty. Her expression blank, her eyes red and swollen, she brushed a hank of blond hair off her forehead then dropped her hands to her lap, raising her gaze to Risa's at the same time.

They'd talked only briefly at Christmas parties and the like. Not sure Luke's wife would recognize her, Risa went to her knees and put her hands over Melinda's. Too late, she remembered the dried blood that still painted her fingers. Melinda didn't seem to notice.

"I'm so sorry," Risa said, her voice cracking despite herself. "I tried to stop them, Melinda, I swear. I—I just wasn't fast enough."

She blinked at Risa with eyes as pale as her hair. "I'm sure you did all that could be done." Her words were spoken as if by rote, dully and in a chopped-up fashion.

Risa didn't quite know what she'd expected from Melinda, but this wasn't it. Grief, for sure, anger, perhaps? She pondered the question for a second then suddenly realized the obvious: Melinda was doped to her eyeballs, which was probably a good idea, Risa decided.

"I'm sorry," Risa repeated. "If there's anything I can do…"

As Melinda nodded, Risa began to rise but she was pulled back abruptly, Melinda gripping her stained fingers to hold her still. "Did he say anything?" she whispered.

Risa looked into her tortured eyes and made an instant decision, lying without hesitation. "He said he loved you and Jason."

A momentary confusion flickered over Melinda Rowling's face, then it was gone.

Without another word, she released Risa's hands. Her emotions in chaos, her cheek now throbbing, Risa stood unsteadily then turned to leave. The uniformed men parted silently as the five women walked through them. After they passed, the path behind them closed once more and the vigil resumed.

THE WOMEN WALKED Risa to the hospital's lobby, arguing over who would spend the night with her. She let them yak until they reached the elevator for the parking garage.

"No one's staying with me," she said firmly. "I need a ride home and then I'll be fine."

Abby looked at her with worried eyes. "You can't be by yourself tonight, Risa. You're been through too much to be alone."

Mei Lu concurred. "You need company."

"I'll be fine," Risa repeated, "and besides, I want to be alone. I need to think about everything that happened."

"But that's the problem," Crista replied. "You'll think too much and get even more upset." She stepped to Risa's side and put her arm around her shoulder, squeezing her gently.

As usual, Lucy was the lone dissenter. "Come on, you guys, Risa knows what she's talking about. Let's let her work this out like she wants to. I think that's for the best."

The others looked uncertain but, one by one, agreed, albeit reluctantly. Exchanging a final hug, they went their separate ways, Crista the one elected to drive Risa home. They headed down an almost deserted Main Street, winding through Rice University until they came out at the freeway again.

Crista glanced in her rearview mirror then over at Risa. "You did the right thing tonight, so I hope you don't start second-guessing what happened."

"I won't," Risa said woodenly.

"Yes, you will," Crista replied. "You already are. I heard what you said to Melinda."

"I didn't know what else to say." Risa stared blindly out the window at the passing buildings. "I had to say something."

"So you're okay with how it went down?"

"I'm okay with it."

The rest of the twenty-minute drive was silent until they pulled into the driveway of the modest town house Risa had bought the year before. She said, "Thank you," and started to climb out, but Crista's voice stopped her.

"You better prepare yourself, Risa. This could get rough, you know. I've seen the system chew up and spit out a lot of folks, and sometimes the truth gets lost in the process, especially when the IA guys get involved."

"I know there'll be a dog-and-pony show, but I'll get through it. I'm a cop's daughter—remember?"

As the words left her mouth, Risa winced. God, her father... He was sure to know what had happened by now. He was even more connected since he'd retired than he had been in the past; he heard the department's latest gossip before Risa.

"All I'm saying is you have to look out for yourself, okay? No one else is going to do it for you."

Risa stepped out of the car then glanced back through the open window. "I'll be all right."

Crista nodded then Risa turned and went up the sidewalk, the Jeep's lights shining on her as she unlocked the door. Inside the sanctuary of her home,

she closed her eyes and lay her head against the front
door, a weariness sweeping over her that quickly
found a path all the way down to her bones. Her eyes
were dry, though. She wouldn't cry, because she
couldn't. She'd been just a child when her last tear
had been shed and she could still remember her father's mocking voice as it had slid down her cheek.
"Buck up, Risa! Taylors never cry."

"Taylors never cry," she repeated softly in the
dark. As if waiting for an answer, she paused, but
there wasn't one, so she straightened and walked into
the kitchen, going directly to the refrigerator. She
wasn't a big drinker, but she kept some beer on hand
for her friends. Pulling a Tecate out, she popped the
can open and was lifting it to her mouth when the
phone on the wall rang shrilly.

"Ed Taylor, Senior" flashed across the caller ID
screen, and her hand hesitated over the receiver. Two
more rings sounded before she picked it up.

She said hello and her father answered her, his
gruff greeting followed by a heavy, accusatory silence. She hated the games he played and usually
she fought them, but tonight Risa didn't have the
strength. Something about life-and-death situations
took it right out of you, she guessed.

"You heard the news," she said into the void.
"Thanks for calling to check on me."

Her voice held a tinge of sarcasm, but like always,

her father ignored it. "Bobby told me what happened."

Bobby was his former partner, and he was as attached to his police scanner as he was the oxygen tank he had to drag everywhere, years of cigarettes catching up with him. Risa had been surprised her father hadn't come down with cancer himself, just from sharing a cop car with the guy all that time.

"Well, Bobby's always got the goods." She could hear her father's television in the background. It stayed on 24/7. "I guess you know everything, then."

"I know you're alive and your partner isn't." He stopped there, his unspoken censure obvious.

Your brothers wouldn't have gotten themselves into this kind of situation. I always knew something like this was going to happen. You're supposed to back up your partner, not get him shot. What the hell have you done now, Risa?

She had never measured up. And she never would.

Swallowing her defensiveness, she gave him the details, leaving out Luke's inebriation. Her father would be the last one to let it slip, but if the truth got out, Risa feared Luke's family might be in danger of losing all they had left now—his pension. Should the medical examiner run a drug-and-alcohol scan, which he probably wouldn't without cause, then the chips could fall where they did, but Risa wasn't going to bring the subject up.

"I've got it under control," she concluded tightly. "You don't have anything to worry about."

"I don't have anything to worry about regardless," he answered. "This is your bag, Risa. You gotta carry it by yourself."

"Yeah, well, I wouldn't want to do anything to make the family look bad." Her father had left the force with all the right medals pinned to his chest, and her brothers were equally well regarded. The four of them were known as cop's cops. Risa lightened her tone. "Gotta keep the Taylor rep, you know."

He spoke without hesitating, his criticism slicing her heart in two. "I think it's too damn late to worry about that now."

CHAPTER THREE

NOON HAD COME and gone when Grady Wilson wheeled his two-year-old Porsche Boxster into the police headquarters parking garage and made his way up the ramps to his assigned spot. The car was his only extravagance, but he frequently left it at home for weeks at a time, driving an old Volvo to work instead. Sometimes it wasn't worth putting up with the gibes he got whenever one of the guys saw him in the Porsche. This morning he'd decided he didn't really give a big rat's ass.

Picking up the Taylor/Rowling file from the seat next to him, Grady rubbed his eyes and sat for a second. He'd stayed up all night, reading the records he'd downloaded after coming home, and he felt like hell. When this case was over, he should head somewhere down in the islands, like Jamaica. He needed a break. Maybe he needed a permanent break.

Locking the car, he reached the elevator and punched the recall button, thinking of Trudie, his ex. Seven years ago she'd walked into his office late one night and said he was married to the job so he didn't need her, and she'd left. She hadn't given him a chance to defend himself, but that hadn't really mattered, because she'd been right.

And nothing had changed since then. Grady still didn't have a life outside of work. He was forty, but he felt like a hundred. He couldn't remember when he'd had his last date, and he was daydreaming more and more, his mind wandering when it should have been concentrating. Sometimes he imagined himself as one of the monkeys he'd studied while getting his Ph.D. They'd literally worked themselves to death for the food pellets he and his first-year psych students would give them.

Grady continued to labor as hard as the animals had, but the satisfaction that had once made the sacrifices worthwhile was nothing but a memory now. He wasn't quite sure how it had happened, but that had definitely become the case.

After getting a cup of coffee, he went to his office and dropped the file on his desk. He was on the twentieth floor and the view was incredible, but he didn't glance at it as the file on his desk fell open to Taylor's photo. He sipped his coffee and stared at the picture instead.

When he'd gotten to the hospital last night, Risa Taylor had already left, but if she matched the photo in front of him, she was a knockout, no doubt about it. Dark hair, even darker eyes. A body that looked fit and trim. Expanding on his former fantasy—and it *was* a fantasy because he knew he'd never take that vacation—he mentally gave her a bikini and put her on his Jamaican beach. He was slipping his arm around her bare shoulder when Richards knocked on the door and startled him. Grady cursed loudly as hot coffee splashed over the photo then dripped onto his newest Cole Haans.

"Whoa, man, settle down!" His boss looked at him with disgust. "What's wrong with you?"

Grady rolled his eyes and grabbed a tissue from the box sitting on the corner of the desk, propping his foot up on the edge to dab at his shoes. "Did you need something?"

"I want to know where you are with the Taylor thing. Any thoughts yet?"

He looked up. "For God's sake, Stan, they haven't even had time to mop up the blood. Gimme a break—"

"Okay, okay," the other man said. "I'm just checking, that's all. Don't get your panties in a wad. I'm asking for the mayor."

God, first the chief, now the mayor. Who was next? The governor?

Grady continued to brush at his shoes. "You can tell the mayor I'll let you know what I know after I talk to Taylor and find out what she knows."

Richards knew better than to press Grady—he had

his own way of doing things and had never played by the book—but Richards didn't expect a real answer anyway. All he wanted was the ability to report back to his superiors that he had asked. He fled as Grady took another swipe at his loafers then tossed the tissue, wondering again about the role of the higher-ups in the situation. Maybe Stan hadn't been lying about Chief Tanner. Knowing there was only one way to find out for sure, Grady picked up the sopping file and headed for Risa Taylor's office.

After several false starts—navigation was not his strong suit—Grady found the Sex Crimes offices. An older woman with neatly braided hair looked up as he entered their area. Her name tag read, "Debra Figer," and she'd been crying—her eyes were rimmed with red and glistening.

Grady introduced himself, but left out his department. "I'm here to see Risa Taylor—"

"She didn't come in today." The woman pursed her lips. Grady didn't recognize her but she seemed to know who he was. "She was wounded last night and the boss told her to stay home."

Grady nodded with a pleasant expression and started back down the hall. As he turned the corner, he heard Figer pick up her phone and punch out a number.

Before he could return to his office, Risa Taylor

would know he was looking for her. He pulled his car keys from his pocket and walked quickly down the corridor.

GINGERLY TOUCHING the bandage on her cheek, Risa stared into her bathroom mirror then reached for the vial of pain pills on the counter. She regretted not taking the sleeping pills the doc had offered, but she didn't handle that kind of stuff too well. Her cheek felt as if it'd been branded, though, and she had to do something. Shaking out one of the capsules, she broke it in two, then paused, her mind wandering.

When he'd gotten to the scene last night, Luis Trevino, her boss, had ordered her to stay home today. She'd ignored his words and had been getting ready when he'd called her earlier that morning.

"Take off the suit and forget about it," he'd said when she'd answered the phone.

"How did you know I was—"

"I meant what I said last night, Risa. I want you to stay home today and take it easy. We aren't doing anything productive anyway. Everyone's pretty rattled."

"What's the word on the second shooter?"

"He's hanging on, but barely. The docs still won't let us talk to him so we've printed him and we're working on an ID."

"I could come in and help, look at the books or something."

"No. You stay home. That's it. No arguing."

She'd gone back to bed and hadn't woken up until the phone had rung again a half hour ago. This time, Debra had been on the other end and she'd explained about the man who'd been looking for Risa. The secretary seemed to know everyone on the force and she'd been positive the man was IA, but Risa had doubts. Things generally moved slowly at HPD, but the Internal Affairs department was notorious for its glacierlike progress. When Risa looked down at the half pill in her hand, though, she decided to wait. Opening her fingers, she let both pieces of the capsule drop into the sink then she turned on the water to wash them away. If by chance, Debra *was* right, Risa wanted all her wits about her.

Pushing away from the counter, she shuffled downstairs with the vague intention of eating something. She hadn't had anything since lunch the day before, but the thought of food made her stomach churn. She decided on coffee instead. Heating a cup in the microwave from the pot she'd made earlier, she stared out the kitchen window to the small alcove that was her yard.

Last night had been the worst night of her life. She'd tried to sleep, but all she'd done was replay the shooting over and over and over. The few times she'd managed to drift off, she'd jerked herself awake, dodging bullets. If she'd thought she'd have gotten any help, she would have called her dad, but even as desperate as she had been, she'd known better. He'd never thought she'd make it on the force.

And maybe he'd been right, she thought as the microwave dinged and she pulled out her mug. What kind of officer let her partner get shot, point-blank?

The doorbell sounded and Risa jumped, splashing hot coffee down the blue warm-up she'd put on after changing from her suit and going back to bed. Not nearly enough time had passed for Debra's IA man to be here, so the damn reporters had to have returned. Risa cursed and brushed at the stain with a cup towel, then she gave up and tossed it to the countertop, the bell pealing again, this time with more insistence. She'd already told two of them she had nothing to say. Storming into the entry, she jerked the door open with harsh words on her lips.

"Look, I already told you people I wasn't saying anything."

A man stood on the front porch. She didn't know who he was, but he was not a reporter or a cop. His suit was too expensive and there were no cameras behind him or vans in the driveway. There *was* a Porsche, however. Her eyes came back to his. They were the color of cold ashes and she shivered without thinking.

"Risa Taylor?" His voice was deep and smooth, a direct contrast to the chill in his stare.

"I'm Grady Wilson." He held out his hand and she shook it. "A lieutenant with HPD Internal Affairs."

Risa's stomach tightened, and she sucked in her breath. So much for her policewoman's judgment. Score one for Debra.

"May I come in?" he asked.

"Of course." She stepped aside and he brushed past her. He was tall, well over six feet, and he made her five-six height feel insignificant.

"Please sit down." She waved toward her living room. "Would you like some coffee? I just spilled half a pot down my pants, but I think there's some left."

He made a wry face then lifted his right foot. His leather shoe—also expensive—was freshly spotted with something dark. "I'm wearing my caffeine today, too," he replied. "But I'd like to have some to drink, if it's not any trouble."

She nodded. "No problem. Give me a minute."

Back in her kitchen, Risa made fresh coffee, her nerves zinging. She couldn't believe the guy had gotten here so quickly. He was obviously a fast worker...and a fast driver. Watching the first drips of coffee flow into the thermal pot, she tried to talk herself out of being anxious, but she failed.

She put everything on a tray and returned to the

living room, sitting down on the couch. "How do you take your coffee, Lieutenant?"

He turned away from the photos hanging above her fireplace. "Black is fine, and frankly, I'd rather you call me Grady."

She filled a cup and held it out to him as he walked toward the sofa, his request surprising her. "Are you sure?" she asked skeptically.

He smiled in a friendly way and took the coffee. "I always drink it black."

She shook her head. "I'm talking about the lieutenant part."

He sat down right beside her. His closeness made her feel uncomfortable, but if he realized it, he pretended he didn't. Then again, she thought abruptly, maybe that was exactly why he'd sat where he did.

"I may be in Internal Affairs, Officer Taylor, but I'm not immune to what the rank and file think about my division. I find it more helpful if we try not to get too stuffy during these kinds of investigations."

He took a swallow of coffee then looked at her over the mug, his strange gray eyes measuring her in a manner that left her even more apprehensive than his proximity. "If the laxity makes you ill at ease, feel free to use the title."

It did just that, but she wasn't about to let him know.

"Grady is fine," she answered.

"You were wounded." He smoothly changed gears and nodded toward her bandage. "How do you feel today? Are you in any pain?"

"I'm okay. I would have gone in but my boss wouldn't let me." She touched the patch briefly. "It's nothing."

"But the loss of your partner isn't."

Her eyes went to her hands, which were wrapped around her coffee mug. She'd scrubbed them for a long time last night, removing Luke's blood. The red stains had washed off easily, too easily, considering what they represented.

"Luke Rowling was a good cop." She lifted her eyes once more to Wilson's. "And a good man. I'll miss him."

"Have you thought about talking to the department shrink? Leo Austen's very professional and he knows his stuff."

"I'd assumed I'd be seeing him at some point during all this," Risa answered. "He's part of the package, isn't he?"

"'The package' varies with each situation, Officer. A lot of what happens next will depend on you." He put his drink down on the table. "For example, you need to decide if you want to contact your union rep before we talk. That's your option, you know."

"I'm not a member of the union."

His dark eyebrows lifted almost imperceptibly.

"I don't need anyone to hold my hand," she said in a dismissive way. "I'm a big girl."

He nodded slowly. "I understand, but sometimes it's nice to have the support." He tilted his head toward the fireplace and the photos. "How about your dad?"

"How about him?"

"Have you talked to him?"

"Yes."

He waited for more, but she gave him nothing.

"What about your friends?"

"They were with me last night."

"What about the chief? I understand you're pretty tight with her."

Her eyes jerked to his. "Catherine Tanner was one of my instructors at the Academy. We are friends, but you can leave that fact out of this equation, Lieutenant."

"I intend to," he said steadily.

He held her gaze for longer than was necessary, then he leaned back and put his arm across the top of the couch. His fingertips were an inch away from her shoulder and he seemed totally relaxed.

"Tell me what happened, Risa. In your own words. At your own pace. I want to hear the whole story and I've got plenty of time."

IT WAS PAST FOUR by the time Risa stopped talking. She'd been tight-mouthed at first, especially since she'd explained everything over and over the night before, then his gray eyes had warmed and she'd relaxed. Relating the same story to Grady Wilson somehow felt different. For one thing, he was an excellent listener, and for another, he knew the right kind of questions to ask. She'd almost forgotten he was an IA guy—she'd felt as if she were talking to a friend instead.

Which was probably a big mistake on her part.

She looked at the man still sitting on her couch. At some point she'd risen from the cushions and walked to the other side of the room. He was in the same relaxed position.

"Anything else?" he asked.

"I think that's it. I did everything by the book, but I know there's a world of difference between sustained and exonerated."

If he found the first, she could face criminal charges. Needless to say her career would be over. If he found the second, her record would stay pristine.

No one except the IA guys themselves understood the mazelike paths their investigations could take, and rumor had it, even some of them got lost on occasion. A lot of officers, especially the union guys, felt the obfuscation was deliberate, but Risa wasn't sure. All she knew for certain was that Grady Wilson was in charge of what would happen next. He could recommend more training and counseling for Risa, but written reprimands, a suspension or even termination were options, as well.

Whatever he decided, after his investigation he'd present his recommendation to his boss who would, in turn, hand it over to the assistant chief of IA. The assistant chief and the Citizens' Review Committee would examine everything then the chief would get her chance.

Catherine would make the final determination. She could send the case to the district attorney and a grand jury if criminal charges were to be filed or she could dismiss the whole affair. Either way, she counted on the IA investigator. Nine times out of ten, his original suggestion became the final outcome.

Everything depended on Grady Wilson.

"Whatever the results," he said, "you can always appeal if you're unhappy."

"I won't be unhappy because I followed department procedures. It happened so fast I didn't have a chance to do anything else."

"That's why your training is so important. Sometimes it's all you have. Your training…and the truth."

They stared at each other from across the room. He seemed to be waiting for her to say something else. Finally, after several more seconds, he stood and reached inside his coat, removing a business card that he dropped to her coffee table.

"That has all my numbers on it," he said. "Home, cell, office, whatever. If you think of anything else you'd like me to know, don't hesitate to call, 24/7."

"I've told you everything," she answered, "but I'm sure we'll be talking more."

He murmured, "Oh, yes," then followed her as she led him back to the entry.

Despite the smoothness of the interview, Risa still felt anxious as she opened the front door. Grady took a step toward the threshold then stopped. They stood close, almost eye to eye, and her gaze went to his hair. It was thick and longer than she'd thought, curling at the base of his neck. More than one strand was gray, but she found that reassuring—he wasn't a rookie. She also found it strangely sexy.

"When you come back to the office, we'll start the paperwork," he said, "but it may take a few days. Be prepared for delays."

She frowned and focused once more. "Delays?"

"You know how it is," he answered with an easy smile. "Forms to get the forms to get the forms. It's all routine and the whole deal won't last long, even though it might feel differently."

Risa stilled. "I don't think I understand," she said slowly. "What's routine and won't last long?"

His eyes met hers, and she suddenly wondered why she'd thought them warm.

"I assumed you knew," he said quietly. "Until this situation has been cleared, you'll be behind a desk."

RISA TAYLOR'S EYES WIDENED until Grady felt himself enveloped by their darkness.

"That's crazy!" she blurted out. "I know it's the rule but I can't sit on my butt while this investigation is ongoing! My partner's dead! I'm not going to stay on the bench while everyone else is out there doing their best—"

"Your team will understand," Grady said calmly. "This is SOP for an officer-involved shooting."

"I don't give a damn what's standard." Her expression was fierce, energy vibrating around her like sound waves off a tuning fork. "This is different! I *have* to do something."

"You don't have a choice in this matter, Officer Taylor." Grady stared at her, the sympathy he felt for her well hidden. "You're off the beat—and the case—until this investigation is resolved. Homicide will be handling it."

"But I can help!"

"Your cooperation will be necessary, yes, but not as an officer. You were a participant and, as such, you can't work the case, too. Surely you understand that?''

"Well, of course I do, but this situation is different.''

"It seems that way because it's happened to you, but all I can say is I'm sorry. I do know how you feel.''

"I doubt that.'' She looked at him with open animosity. "Not unless you've lost a partner, too.''

He started to tell her the truth, something he hadn't done with anyone in a very long time, but he swallowed his answer. Stepping off her porch and into the sunlight, he said, "Call me when you decide to return to headquarters, Officer Taylor. I'll be waiting.''

CHAPTER FOUR

Luis Trevino phoned Risa that evening.

"Everybody's bugging the hell outta me to find out how you're doin' so I thought I'd better call. You okay or what?"

Risa couldn't help but smile. "Thanks for the concern, boss. Knowing you care so much makes me feel really loved."

He made a sound between a snort and a chuckle, then spoke again. "Just answer the question, Taylor."

Her fingers went to her bandage. "I'm okay. I'm coming in tomorrow."

"No, you're not," he replied. "We got a new rule on the books. Injured officers gotta stay home for at least two days."

"Forget it. I'm coming in. I want to work. It's better for me than sitting here and thinking."

"Yeah, thinking can be dangerous," he conceded. "But I don't want you back yet. You, ah, need to rest some more."

He was bullshitting her. She waited a second before answering. "What's going on, Luis?"

The silence continued until he broke it with a
curse. "The IA prick, Wilson, came in this afternoon
and told me there's some kinda holdup with your file.
Nothing important, just some bureaucracy crap."

"It's okay," she said. "You shoulda just said so
in the first place."

"I knew you wouldn't be happy about it."

"It's part of the deal, Luis. I understand how it's
going to work. You don't need to baby me."

"I'm not," he said defensively.

"Yes, you are," she countered. "But that's okay,
too. Maybe I could stand a little babying, whether I
want it or not."

"I'm glad you're not mad at me 'cause tomorrow's going to be bad enough as it is." He hesitated
as if he wasn't sure of her reaction to what he was
going to say next. "They've scheduled the memorial
service, Risa. Two o'clock, Settlegast-Kopf on
Kirby, day after tomorrow. Later on, there's gonna
be a private cremation."

Later on... Risa swallowed as she realized what
Luis meant. An autopsy had to be performed and
Luke's body could not be buried until those results
were in. They talked for a few more minutes about
the status of her cases, then they hung up. Closing

her eyes, Risa put her head down on the kitchen table.

But she didn't cry.

She thought instead.

She thought about Luke and his kid. She thought about her and her father. Finally she thought about Grady Wilson, or, as Luis had put it so succinctly, the IA prick.

Grady had told her to be prepared for delays, but what did it matter now? When she did get back, she was going to be stuck behind a desk instead of doing anything worthwhile.

Her mind struggled to cope with the chaos that had taken over her life. Yesterday morning—a little more than twenty-four hours ago—Risa had had everything in order: her future, her career, her very existence—and now nothing but anarchy ruled. Her partner was dead, she was under investigation and her job had just disappeared. For one crazy minute, she had the feeling that she might just follow.

She cursed Grady Wilson, then she took a deep breath.

The guy was simply doing his job, just as she'd told everyone he was. Nothing more. Nothing less.

The situation was only temporary. In a matter of days, if not weeks, the IA man with the spooky eyes would conclude his investigation and Risa would return to the street and do what she'd been trained to do. Instead of whining, she should be on her knees thanking God. Eventually, she'd have her life back.

Luke wouldn't.

GRADY TOOK a final look in the mirror and straightened his Windsor knot one more time. He'd come home after a late lunch to change for the memorial service. He got as much grief over his clothes as he did his car, but he liked being well dressed. It was a throwback to his peanut-butter-sandwich days. When he'd been a kid, and later on a starving student, he'd promised himself he'd dress well when he got older, even if he didn't have the money. People believed what they saw, and if they saw someone who looked successful, they thought he *was* successful.

Grady knew better, of course. He'd worked IA too damn long to believe anything, including his own eyes, but most people hadn't witnessed all he had.

Turning away from the mirror, Grady walked down the hall of his two-bedroom house. He lived in the Heights, an eclectic, historic area off the Katy Freeway. The neighborhood was perpetually ''in transition'' as the architects put it, commercial property next to homes and vice versa, each one fluctuating wildly in value. Trudie had insisted on living there, though, and she'd financed the place. It'd been way out of bounds for Grady's salary, but by that point, he hadn't cared. He'd let her have her way and when she'd left him, he'd paid her off, getting a loan on the side. The community had grown on him but it wasn't for everyone.

Risa Taylor lived in a completely opposite milieu. An organized enclave of town homes and condos, her part of Houston had restrictions and fences and manicured lawns with scheduled maintenance. If everything in her file was the truth, and he had no reason to believe it wasn't, then her surroundings fit her as well as his own did him. He was willing to bet serious money she had always colored between the lines as a child.

Grady reminded himself as he backed out of his driveway that he shouldn't be making hasty judgments about the people he was investigating. He'd attended a seminar last year about sensitivity in IA matters, where they'd all been admonished to keep an open mind and let the natural traits of the officers reveal themselves. Don't jump to conclusions, their instructor had instructed. Police intuition is the stuff of TV series, she'd pronounced.

Grady had pronounced *her* theories "bullshit" and had walked out. He'd always depended on his gut and he wasn't about to start doing anything different now. Especially not with Risa Taylor.

He *knew* she was what he had already decided she was—an honest, conservative cop, too bright to be on the force but too dedicated to leave. Her actions the other night had most likely saved her life, though not her partner's. She'd done what she had to in order to survive and Grady was ninety-nine percent sure he could investigate her until the end of time and he wouldn't find anything to the contrary.

On the other hand...

That one percent did exist and he knew it did because he'd been bitten on the ass by it before. Also, there was something about Risa Taylor that bothered him. She seemed like a pretty together person yet he couldn't shake the feeling that underneath the polished exterior something more existed. For lack of a better word, he'd defined it as "energy." A ferocious, determined and potentially dangerous kind of energy. If she didn't keep it under control, it might end up controlling her. He'd seen too many cops who had gone to the other side in the war they were all fighting because they couldn't handle themselves.

He swung into the right-hand lane and took the exit for the Loop 610. Traffic was bad. The late-lunch crowd was still on the road and the sneaking-out-early guys had begun to join them. By the time he got to Kirby he was almost late.

Despite that fact, after parking the Volvo, he sat for a moment and watched the mourners cross the funeral home's parking lot. The majority of them were cops and Grady couldn't help but wonder which one of them would phone him. In every investigation, someone contacted him about halfway into the case with a tip. The caller was always anonymous and always a cop, but not always helpful.

From the corner of his eye, he saw Risa Taylor approaching. Talking to four other women, she passed directly in front of his car. She didn't recognize the Volvo, of course, so Grady took the opportunity to study her.

Straight black hair hung almost to her shoulders and it gleamed in the hot sunlight. Her sleeveless dark dress revealed arms that were tanned and muscular. She'd played tennis in college, he remembered from her file, and obviously still did. As she cleared the car, he glanced at her legs. They were tight and firm. As was the rest of her.

He called himself a dirty old man. At twenty-six, Risa could have almost been his daughter had he ever been successful with the girl next door. There were certainly fourteen-year-old kids around now who had babies. He saw them everywhere.

He shook the thought from his head and climbed out of the car.

Five minutes later he was seated two rows behind Risa and her friends. When the service started and everyone rose, Grady stood, too. But he didn't turn around to watch Melinda Rowling and her son approach. Instead, he faced the front so he could see

Risa's reaction as Melinda walked down the center aisle.

Unfortunately, Risa spotted Grady before she saw the widow. Her dark eyes widened and she seemed to catch her breath. One of the women looked at her with a questioning glance, but Risa shook her head at her friend's concern, mouthing the words *it's okay.* From where he stood, Grady read her lips, then found himself distracted by her mouth itself. She had on red lipstick—bright red—yet instead of looking cheap as it would have on most women, the color seemed to be made for her.

The family passed by and he remembered where he was.

Risa looked at Grady one more time. She'd regained her composure and he couldn't have read her expression had his life depended on it.

When he thought about that later, he decided it was probably just as well.

THE DAY AFTER the shooting, Mei Lu had picked up Risa's Camry from the downtown police garage and dropped it off at her house. Risa could have driven to the services, but when Abby had offered her a ride, she'd accepted, surprising herself—and Abby. Usually independent and self-sufficient, Risa still felt nervous, and fighting Houston's traffic was not something she'd wanted to do. As they left the memorial service and headed to the south side of town where Luke Rowling had lived, Risa found herself even more grateful. She wasn't sure she would have made it on her own, especially after seeing Grady Wilson at the services.

She'd actually trembled when her eyes had connected with his and she had no idea why. Except for what he did, he seemed like a perfectly nice man. She decided to blame her reaction on the pain pill she'd taken before leaving the house.

Behind the wheel, Abby worried. "I wish everyone else was coming. Lucy said she had something going with a case, though, and Crista had some kind of meeting planned. Mei Lu didn't say why she wouldn't be there. Did Catherine tell you if she'd be at Luke's?"

Risa's thoughts drifted back to Grady Wilson then she realized Abby was asking her something. For the second time.

"Risa? Have you heard from her?"

"From who?"

"From Catherine..." Abby shot her an anxious glance. "Will she be at the Rowlings'?"

Risa shook her head. "Debra said she stopped by earlier this morning because she was going to give the press a statement after the services." She turned back to the window.

Abby reached across the seat and touched her arm.

When Risa looked over, Abby asked, "Are you okay?"

Risa's answer was *not really* but she said, "I'm fine."

"Do you want to talk about it?"

Risa smiled affectionately at her friend. She was lucky to have Abby and all the others, but like her father had said, this was an ordeal Risa was going to have to go through alone.

"There's nothing to talk about, Abby. Luke is dead and for the moment, my hands are tied. I want to help with the investigation, but I can't. End of story."

Switching topics, Abby kept the conversation light after that, Risa answering her occasional question by rote. Just as they pulled to the curb outside Luke's house, Abby's cell phone chirped. Risa stepped out while Abby took the call and a second later, still behind the wheel, Abby rolled down the window closest to Risa and called out her name.

Risa bent down to look at her. "What's up?"

Abby's face was wreathed in concern. "I've got to go. The team's had a call—a jumper's threatening to go off the Ship Channel Bridge and it's all hands on deck. I hate to strand you like this but I don't know what else to do."

"Forget about it. I'll find a way home, don't worry."

"Are you sure?"

"Of course I'm sure," Risa answered. "If nothing else, I can call a cab." She made a dismissive motion with her hand. "Go on. Duty's calling."

Abby nodded and pulled back out to the street, her car disappearing in a haze of heat a minute later. Risa smoothed her dress and started up the sidewalk. Abby's support would have been great, but until she'd attended the Academy and met everyone else, Risa had never been close to anyone. Her father and brothers had seemed to share some kind of testosterone-laden pact she'd been left out of, and with no mother or even an aunt nearby to compensate for it, Risa had had to make do on her own. Meeting Abby and Mei Lu, Crista and Lucy, Risa had finally learned what it meant to have friends. Catherine's success had cemented the group, giving them inspiration as well.

David Kinner opened the Rowlings' front door before the doorbell could finish its peals. Sucking in her breath, Risa stifled her reaction as the overweight cop scowled then led her to a white satin guest book. When she finished signing the book, he pointed toward the back of the house, his attitude cold and indifferent.

"Everyone's in the living room," he said. "There's coffee and cake in the dining room."

There were over seven thousand law enforcement

officers in Harris County. Why had Melinda chosen
Kinner to stand at the front door and greet everyone?
She'd probably asked him to help since he'd been on
Luke's team. Certainly not for his charming ways.

Risa put him out of her mind and walked down
the hall.

Five feet down the narrow corridor, she found the
dining area. A tiny space to begin with, the crowd
made it seem even smaller. All she could see was
wall-to-wall uniforms, then Debra appeared at her
side. Taking Risa's elbow, the secretary pulled her
out of the stream of people and into a nearby corner.

Risa shook her head. "My God, Debra, what a
crowd!"

"I know it. Been this way since this morning. So
many people have come by, there hasn't been room
to swing a cat." She reached out and plucked a plate
off the laden dining-room table, handing it to Risa.
"Get yourself something, then let's go into the other
room. There are less folks in there."

Risa held her hand up, the thought of food curling
her stomach into a knot. "I'm not hungry," she said.
"But escaping this mob sounds like a good idea. You
lead the way, I'll follow."

Replacing the plate, Debra turned around to push
a path through the crowd. They came out in the comparative serenity of the kitchen. Stuffed with cabinets
and open shelves full of knickknacks, the area was

actually smaller, but there were fewer people in it. Risa focused on the wall beside the refrigerator, a framed photograph of Jason catching her attention.

Following her stare, Debra spoke softly. "Poor little guy. It's hell to be that young and not have a daddy no more."

Risa's throat tightened. "Is he here?"

"I haven't seen him. I think I heard someone say a neighbor lady's got him."

A few months ago, his car in the shop, Luke had asked Risa for a ride home. After she'd eased into his driveway, the front door had shot open and his son had barreled out, Melinda right behind him. He'd been yelling something about a cartoon show. When Luke had scooped him up and kissed him, Risa had seen the kind of love shining from his eyes that she had always wanted—but never received—from her own old man.

"Where's Melinda?" she asked.

"In there." Debra nodded toward an open area off the kitchen. "She's sittin' on the couch. Looking bad, too."

Risa knew she should go into the living room and give her condolences to Luke's wife, but her feet wouldn't move. Not understanding her reluctance but yielding to it all the same, Risa stayed where she was, listening to Debra. After a while, when it seemed as if they'd been interrupted a hundred times,

Risa came to the realization that almost everyone present had stopped and spoken to her, some briefly, some not so briefly. Despite the lingering prejudice in the department, these men understood, in a way no one else could, the relationship between partners. The widow had lost her husband, but Risa had lost someone important, too. Their support bolstered her and after half an hour or so, she put her hand on Debra's arm, finally halting the secretary's nonstop flow of words.

"I think I should go talk to Melinda." Risa nodded toward the living room. "You want to come with me?"

Debra said, "Of course," and the two of them started forward. The crowd had thinned a bit but not much. They were directly in front of the sofa before Risa even saw Melinda. She wore a shapeless navy dress with a white collar, the pale lace at her neck accentuating her pallor, the dark fabric drawing attention to the bruised shadows beneath her eyes. A uniformed officer sat beside her, her hand in his as he patted her back and murmured something. He could have been a model with his blue eyes and thick blond hair. Risa looked closely at him, but she failed to come up with a name as Debra pulled her forward.

"Melinda?" Debra bent over and gently touched the woman's shoulder. "Risa's here," she announced. "She wants to visit with you, honey."

The man beside Melinda stood and started to speak but before he could, Melinda jumped to her feet, screaming.

"What do you think you're doing here? I can't believe you'd show your face in my house!" As if to attack Risa, the woman lurched forward with both hands in the air. "My husband would still be alive if it weren't for you! He loved me and you took him from me!"

Dismayed at Melinda's words and shocked by her action, Risa gasped and tried to reverse her steps. She didn't get far. In the crowded room, her back hit someone's chest and she stumbled. She lost her balance and started to fall.

A second later Melinda was on top of her, her fists pounding, her nails scratching. She continued to scream incoherently and all Risa could do was duck.

"THAT'S ENOUGH!"

"C'mon, stop it!"

The cops nearest the two women sprang into action, but Melinda continued to pummel Risa. From across the room, Grady, who'd only arrived a few moments before, heard the commotion then cursed when he saw what was happening. Pushing his way through the crowd, he stepped between the two women and thrust Risa behind him. Their eyes met briefly; she looked terrified and completely confused.

Separated from the target of her anger, Melinda let her hysteria morph into noisy sobbing. She tried one more time to lunge forward, but the officers contained her and she collapsed into a heap on the sofa, disappearing behind a wall of blue.

Grady took Risa's hand and pulled her from the room.

They didn't stop until they were outside.

Risa looked over her shoulder toward the house, blinked several times, then turned to him, her eyes dark with disbelief. "What in the hell was that?"

"I don't know." Grady kept his expression neutral. "She did seem upset, didn't she?"

Risa's eyebrows lifted into perfect twin arches. "Upset? I think she was speeding past upset and heading straight for hysterical."

He played the psychiatrist. "People handle grief a lot of different ways."

"That wasn't grief," she said flatly. "She was pissed, big time."

"Why do you say that?"

Risa gave him what Grady called "The Look." He'd never known a woman who didn't have it in her repertoire of expressions, but his ex had been a master at it. Big eyes, curled lips, slightly tilted head. Its meaning was simple: *Are you really that big of an idiot?*

"Why?" Risa repeated. "Why? Maybe because she just tried to beat the crap out of me!"

She trembled as she spoke, but with fear or with anger? He couldn't tell.

"It's a natural reaction," he said, "if somewhat dramatic. She has to blame someone for Luke's death. You were handy."

Risa shook her head. "She didn't feel that way the night of the shooting."

"How do you know?"

"She said so at the hospital. I made a point of speaking to her before I went home. I told her..." Pausing, Risa licked her lips and took a breath then continued. "I told her I had tried my best and she said she knew I'd done all that I could. What happened between then and now?"

Grady was pretty sure he knew, but he kept the information to himself.

"She was probably in shock," he said instead.

"She was out of it. You could have driven a truck through her pupils."

"The doctors must have given her something."

"Maybe. Maybe not."

Her answer was too ambiguous to let slide. "What does that mean?" He paused, an idea forming before he could stop it. "Did Luke Rowling use drugs, Risa?"

Her dark eyes shot to his. "Why do you ask?"

"You just implied his wife might. Chances are good that if she does, he did."

"I'm not sure I agree with your logic." Her voice was stiff, her spine the same. "But to answer your question, Luke didn't use drugs, as far as I knew."

Something about the way she said the word *drugs* tugged at Grady's brain.

Her abrupt announcement gave him no time to figure out why. "I'm wiped out," she said. "I'm going home. I've had enough of this for one day."

She opened her purse and removed a cell phone instead of a set of keys, punching the buttons almost angrily. When she asked for the number of a taxi service, Grady reached over and took the unit from her shaking hands, closing it gently.

"I'll take you home," he said. "There's no need for that."

"A friend of mine brought me, but she was called out the minute we got here." She took her phone back and began to dial again. "I can get a cab... there's no point in troubling you."

He closed her phone one more time. "It's on my way," he lied. "I insist."

She started to argue but stopped and tottered slightly. Grady took both her elbows in his hands. "Whoa, whoa," he said. "You okay?"

Before she could answer, he noticed her bandage. This was a new one, smaller and less conspicuous than what she'd worn right after the shooting, but in the scuffle, one corner of the tape holding it down had come undone.

"I'm fine," she said faintly. "It's just the…the pain pill I took. I don't do so well on meds."

Grady lifted his hand to Risa's cheek and smoothed the small dressing back into place. Her skin was unbelievably soft and almost transparent and he wondered what it would taste like. His fingers lingered a little longer than they should have.

"I'm fine," she repeated.

He wanted to say *You certainly are,* but something told him she might not appreciate the compliment right now. He dropped his hand.

"My car's right here." He nodded toward the other side of the street. "Let's get you home."

CHAPTER FIVE

HE WALKED her up the sidewalk, took her keys and unlocked the front door. Half worried she might pass out on him, Grady put his hand firmly in the center of Risa's back and directed her into the entryway ahead of him.

She made it to her sofa then sank down. Grady took off his coat and found his way to her kitchen, where he filled a glass with cold water then brought it back to her.

She took the tumbler with shaking hands. "Thank you," she said. "I don't know what's wrong with me."

"Getting shot makes some folks a little woozy. Everything's just hitting you at once. I'm not surprised." He perched on the edge of her coffee table and stared at her. The paleness of her complexion made her eyes look even darker. He waited until she regained some color then he spoke. "If I were you, though, I'd avoid Melinda Rowling for a while."

"Don't worry, I will. She might come after me

with something besides her fingernails next time. I don't need any more scars.''

He found himself reaching over to touch the bandage on her cheek. Again. ''Does it hurt?''

She blinked then shook her head. ''Not really. Not like I thought it would.'' Looking into the glass she held, she stayed silent for a bit, then she raised her gaze to his. ''The wound isn't my problem. And the pills probably aren't, either. It's just the whole...the whole damn thing.''

''Losing a partner is hard.''

Her expression went thoughtful, and he braced himself as she spoke. ''You've been through this yourself, haven't you?''

Grady wasn't the kind of guy who lay in bed at night and worried about what should have been instead of what really was. The past was over. He started to lie as he usually did.

Then he stopped.

''Yes, I have,'' he said. ''It's not something I like to talk about.''

''I can certainly understand why.'' She paused. ''But would you mind telling me? It might...help.''

He couldn't say no. Risa Taylor was a woman hard to refuse, no matter what the request.

''I was a beat cop in New York,'' he said quietly. ''I'd been partners with the same guy for almost seven years. During the day, I went to school, and he took care of his kids while his wife worked, so we did the graveyard shift. One night, we caught a domestic in Hell's Kitchen.'' He shook his head, remembering the uselessness of what had followed. ''The call was totally routine, nothing special. We go up the stairs, knock and announce, and the next thing I know there's a Black Talon busting through the door and into my partner's chest. He never knew what hit him.''

Her hand at her throat, Risa seemed to hold her breath. ''Was it an ambush?''

''Nah.'' Grady looked out her living room window to the sidewalk where a kid pushed a bicycle with a flat past the mailbox. ''The perp was aiming for his wife. She was standing by the door but he missed her and got Jimbo instead.''

''I'm sorry.''

''I am, too.'' Their stare held for a moment longer then Grady stood abruptly, suddenly uncomfortable with what he'd shared.

''It happened a long time ago,'' he said in a dismissive way. ''The shooter got stabbed two years into his time and Jimbo's widow remarried six months later.'' He shrugged. ''Life goes on.''

''Are you sure?'' she asked faintly.

''Yeah, I'm sure.'' He took his coat off the chair where he'd dropped it. ''It may not seem like it will, but it does. Eventually.''

"How long does it take to stop hurting?"

"That's one I can't answer." He slipped his arms into his jacket then looked at her. "A lot of years have passed and I'm still waiting."

Grady walked out of the house, closing Risa's front door behind him. He had a hunch her healing time might last a lot longer than his.

He and Jimbo had just been partners.

From what Grady had heard—and apparently Melinda now, too—Risa and Luke had shared more than just the front seat of a cruiser.

Gossip had it they'd shared a bed as well.

THAT WEEKEND, Risa tried to call each of her friends, but Mei Lu was the only one home. They talked for a bit, then after they hung up, with nothing but time on her hands, Risa began to nitpick the entire conversation. In the end, there was nothing she could actually point to and say, "this is it," but in retrospect the chat felt awkward. Mei Lu just hadn't been herself. After thinking about the situation more, Risa decided she hadn't been, either. Her anxiousness had probably rubbed off on her friend and Mei Lu had simply reflected Risa's feelings.

Monday morning a lot of officers stopped her and said something about Luke, but a few seemed cool, too. She puzzled over their attitude then blew it off just as she had Mei Lu's. Whatever the problem was—if it even existed—everything paled in comparison to the fact that she kept expecting to see Luke around every corner. She missed him. The conversation she'd had with Grady about losing his own partner echoed in her mind. He obviously knew what he was talking about, but at the same time, she hoped he was wrong. She couldn't stand the empty, hollow feeling in her gut. If it lasted forever, she was doomed.

She closed her mind to the pain just as she had to Melinda's strange behavior the day before and entered the cubicle Luis had assigned her. The desktop was smooth and completely clear except for the telephone.

For a moment, she panicked. What the hell was she supposed to do all day long? Thankfully, the phone rang just as she dropped her purse into one of the drawers.

Lucy Montalvo's voice made Risa immediately feel better. "You doing okay?"

"I'm hanging on," Risa answered. "But I'm sure glad you called. I'm looking at a very clean desk and eight hours to kill. Why don't I come down and we can run over to Starbucks for a hit?"

"I can't get loose right now," Lucy said, "but I do need to talk to you, if you've got a minute."

"No problem," Risa said. "What's up?"

"I heard about the episode at the Rowlings'," Lucy said. "What was the deal with Melinda?"

"I have no idea." Risa took the chair behind the desk and stared out her door to the wall on the other side of the hall. The cubicle didn't have a window. "I guess it was just an emotional thing, a delayed reaction or something."

Lucy said, "Hmm," and Risa's radar beeped a warning.

"Did you hear something?"

"Not directly," the other woman said. "But you could say I have some news about the situation."

"Someone told you what's going on with her?"

"Maybe."

"C'mon, Luce. What the hell is this?" Risa asked impatiently. "Twenty questions?"

Lucy's voice took on an edge that matched Risa's. "If I were you, I'd be grateful to know whatever came my way, Risa. People have a way of clamming up when things get tough."

Lucy's abruptness wasn't completely out of character, but Risa fell silent. She didn't know what to say.

Apparently neither did Lucy. She was quiet for a moment, then she cursed softly. "Look, I didn't call to give you a hard time, okay? I called because certain people know certain things and they felt you needed to know these things as well. I'm just the messenger.''

Risa stiffened. "Why didn't that person call me and pass on the information directly?"

"Because that person can't."

She understood instantly. "Are you talking about Cath—"

Cutting Risa off, Lucy interrupted her again. "I'm not naming names and neither should you."

Was Lucy implying Risa's line was bugged? She sure as hell hoped not, but an image of Grady Wilson's cold eyes shot into Risa's mind.

"All right, then," Risa said carefully. "What is this all-fired important information?"

"It's gossip," Lucy corrected, "not information. But either way, it's going to hurt you and you need to be prepared." Risa heard her friend draw a breath. "Rumors are being spread that you and Luke were having an affair."

Risa almost laughed, her relief was so great. "Are you kidding me, Luce? God, that's old hat. Surely no one in their right mind thinks that's true."

"Melinda Rowling is the one doing the talking, Risa."

Risa's amusement evaporated.

"And she's making sure people in high places hear her." Lucy paused. "There's more, though."

Her mouth suddenly dry, Risa waited.

"She's telling people you wanted Luke to leave her for you, but he refused—"

"That's crazy."

"And because he rejected you," Lucy continued, as if Risa hadn't spoken, "you took things into your own hands."

"'Took things.' What does that mean?"

"She's saying you killed him."

Risa's throat closed and she couldn't breathe. On the edge of panic, she wondered how long a person could live without air, then her lungs escaped their paralysis and started working again.

"Melinda thinks *I* shot Luke? That's...that's insane! She can't really believe that."

Lucy sounded stiff and strained. "She's told a lot of people she does."

Risa realized she was gripping the telephone with both hands. She forced her fingers to relax, but she couldn't control her heart. It continued to beat way too fast. "God, Lucy, please tell me Cath—" She stopped and started over. "Please tell me no one actually believes this. The idea is completely mental."

"I don't know who believes what right now. Things are getting...complicated."

Since they'd left the Academy, once a month the five women had made it a point to get together and have lunch. Over chicken-salad sandwiches, they'd spent endless hours speculating on the rumors of cor-

ruption within the department. The topic shot into
Risa's mind now, burning its way into her brain without her completely understanding why.

Risa pulled in a sharp breath. "Do you think—"

"I'm not implying that *I* think anything, Risa."
Lucy's voice turned even more curt. "I only called
to pass on the message. Since I've done that, I'll let
you get back to work and I'll do the same."

In a daze, Risa hung up the phone. Debra came
into her cubicle a second later with an armful of files
that she dumped on the desk.

"You wanna clean these out for me? I need to
shred all the pink copies, file the yellow ones, and
send everything else down to the IT department."

Her mind still on the conversation she'd just had
with Lucy, Risa answered with distraction. Only after
Debra walked out of the office did Risa realize she
must have said yes.

In the days since the shooting, Risa had practically
tied her hands behind her back in an effort not to
call Catherine. She knew their friendship could not
interfere with any kind of investigation, but if Melinda Rowling was spreading rumors like this, something had to be done. Risa couldn't allow the woman
to ruin her reputation, much less bring up such serious charges with no proof whatsoever.

Besides that, if Catherine had heard this gossip,
who else knew about it?

Risa's answer came immediately. Maybe that was what had been bothering Mei Lu. It obviously had Lucy on edge.

Then she thought again and her heart stopped. Grady Wilson.

After he'd left yesterday, she'd examined their conversation from every different angle, but she hadn't been able to figure out where he'd been going with his queries. Now it all came together.

Risa pushed her chair away from the desk and headed out the door. She had to find him and explain.

GRADY WAS WALKING out the Travis Street entrance when he heard his name called. He turned, but the double doors had already swung shut and he decided he'd made a mistake. Continuing down the sidewalk, he was stopped a second later by a tug on his jacket. He looked down to see Risa.

A fierce expression darkened her eyes; their angry depths threatened to swallow him up.

"Your secretary told me I might be able to catch up with you if I hurried. We need to talk, Lieutenant Wilson."

Thoughts of Risa had been with him all weekend and he was old enough to know that meant trouble. The kind of trouble that appealed to him greatly. He'd analyzed the situation and come up with the brilliant deduction that her powerful personality and

seductive looks were tinged with just enough vulnerability to make her one of the sexiest women he'd
ever encountered.

"Call me Grady," he said without thinking. "And
I'm sorry, but I'm on my way to district court. I've
got to be there in fifteen minutes."

He started walking again, but she caught up with
him in two paces and this time when she stopped
him her fingers dug into his arm. "I'm sorry, too,
but this can't wait," she persisted. "It's about my
case and it's important."

Pedestrians flowed around the island they made,
separating then coming back together on the other
side.

"I don't know anything new, okay?" he said,
"and even if I did, I can't—"

She pushed at a strand of hair the humidity had
dropped into her eyes. "I just heard about Melinda
Rowling's gossip and I know you've heard it, too.
But there's something you should understand before
you get the wrong idea. It is not true. Not at all."

While her candor surprised him, rules were rules.
He couldn't reciprocate. "Look, I can't talk about
this with you—"

Tightening her fingers, she interrupted him, her
voice softening. "Grady..." She took a breath and
let it out slowly. "Please."

That was all it took.

One word and his name, and he was done, stick a fork in him. He looked down the street with a sigh then brought his gaze back to hers.

"I'll be finished in an hour. Meet me at the tacqueria on San Jacinto at Clay."

A NOONTIME STROLL in the middle of August was not something a sane person did in Houston but, restless with anxiety, Risa walked up one street then down the next, glancing at her watch every five minutes. After half an hour, she found her way to the tiny diner Grady had mentioned and stepped inside. The dark and dingy restaurant felt like a cave, but it was a cool cave, so she took a table and ordered iced tea and chips.

Time slowed to a crawl that matched the speed of the roach going up the wall beside the door. Risa thought about leaving several times, but she had to talk to Grady so she stayed and planned out what she'd say, the words playing inside her head over and over. The idea of her shooting Luke was so ludicrous she didn't even address that part of the issue. The pending autopsy results would prove she hadn't. Melinda had obviously turned unstable in the face of her grief.

The supposed affair, though—that was another thing altogether. Drawing her finger through the circle of water her glass left on the table, Risa shook her head. As far as she'd known, the old gossip about her and Luke had stayed at the station. It hadn't followed him home, she was sure. Who would have been so malicious as to tell Melinda Rowling, and why now of all times? Obviously she'd given the information credence and that's why she'd gone after Risa, but it simply wasn't true.

She thought of her conversations with Mei Lu and Lucy. Surely her friends didn't think she'd hook up with her partner, a married man.

The bell over the door sounded and Risa looked up to see Grady cross the threshold and come toward her table. Waving two fingers to the waiter who was lounging by the double doors of the kitchen, he slid into the seat opposite Risa.

She didn't wait for him to settle in. She went straight to the point. "Look, I need to make sure you don't believe this awful gossip—"

The waiter appeared with two cans of Mexican fruit juice. Grady thanked him in Spanish then ordered the usual for himself and for *la señorita,* as well. Immediately Risa picked up where she'd left off.

"—that Melinda Rowling is spreading. I know you've heard it so let's just cut straight to the chase."

He leaned back in his chair and stared at her. He wore a pair of black-framed glasses he hadn't had on when she'd seen him before and they made him look even more stern. And sexy.

"I am not allowed to discuss ongoing cases, especially with the officers involved in the investigation. Surely you realize that?"

She started to argue then she realized what he'd said. "I don't want to *discuss* the case," she said carefully. "I want to give you some information about it."

He paused. "You can talk all day long if you like. I'm just here to enjoy a nice steaming bowl of *menudo.*"

The waiter reappeared as if on cue and set two plates in front of them, the stew fragrant and hot.

In the face of her growing anxiety, Risa's carefully rehearsed speech disappeared. "It's not the truth," she said bluntly. "What Melinda Rowling is saying about Luke and me. She's lying."

Without giving any indication he'd even heard her, Grady turned to his meal.

She leaned across the table. "It's important you know this," she said. "I did *not* sleep with Luke Rowling. He was a married man *and* a cop. I don't mess with either."

He reached across the table and took a package of crackers from the basket the waiter had left. Opening the cellophane, he nodded and said, "That's good."

His lack of reaction was frustrating. "Do you believe me?" she pressed.

"I have no reason not to." He crumbled the cracker into the bowl and looked up at her again. "Unless you're lying." He paused, his strange-colored eyes steady behind his glasses. "*Are* you lying?"

On the surface of it, his question seemed ridiculous; if she *was* lying, she obviously wouldn't say so. As she stared into his eyes, though, Risa suddenly felt as if she'd been connected to some kind of psychic polygraph machine.

"I have my share of faults," she confessed, "but lying isn't one of them. Especially considering how important this is."

"But that's exactly when most people *do* lie." Mimicking her earlier movement, he leaned closer to the table, his lunch forgotten. "The stakes have to be big, don't they? That's the motivation."

"That may be true," she answered, "but not in this case. Not with me."

He paused for a moment, then said, "All right," but the nervous hole in Risa's gut remained. In fact, it seemed to grow even larger.

He pulled his bowl closer and resumed eating. After two bites, he looked up again and seemed almost surprised to see her still there. "Was there something more?"

Uncomfortable and anxious, she shook her head then stood and started to leave. At the last minute, she paused beside the table. "There is one more thing."

He looked up, his slate eyes unreadable. "Yes?"

"Just for the record, I didn't kill Luke Rowling, either."

CHAPTER SIX

THROUGH THE ROW of windows that lined the tacqueria, Grady watched Risa cross the street. She wore an off-the-rack navy suit that was too big and a blouse that didn't match, but men still stopped and turned to watch her pass. Grady didn't blame them. He would have done the same—hell, he *was* doing the same. Something about the woman demanded your attention. Unless you were blind or dead, you'd take note of Risa Taylor.

Luke Rowling hadn't been blind, but he was dead. Now.

Had she lied to Grady? Had there been an affair? Had she killed him?

Grady took off his glasses and polished them thoughtfully. He hadn't actually believed Melinda Rowling's vicious talk when he'd first heard it and he still wasn't sure he believed it now. Regardless, if Risa Taylor and Luke Rowling had been a couple, their actions would have been stupid but hardly illegal. Of course, nailing the guy was one thing, but killing him was another matter entirely. Still, something about the situation bothered him and he was suddenly afraid that something might be Risa herself.

The thought disturbed him. He finished his stew, threw some bills on the table and walked back to his office.

By Thursday he'd finished the proper forms and conducted most of the necessary interviews. In the process, his file on Risa had grown to over six inches thick, but what was growing even faster was the grapevine. Its tendrils had reached into everyone's office and no matter where Grady went, he heard the rumors being repeated. He knew from experience that even if solid evidence proved otherwise, the salaciousness would continue to spread. It was much more interesting than the truth.

Picking up his phone the following day, Grady punched in Homicide's number and asked for Samuel Andrews, the officer who was handling Rowling's death. The lieutenant came on the phone a few minutes later.

"Just checking in," Grady said. "You got any news for me?"

"I was hoping you might have some for me."

Andrews hadn't heard the gossip. If he had, he would have said so. Grady decided to keep the information to himself, although he didn't know why.

"Not really," he said vaguely. "I'm dicking with

the reports, doing the paper shuffle, that kind of thing. Did the techs ever find any slugs?''

"Not a one," Andrews replied. "That's weird, isn't it?''

"Yeah, but not unheard-of. Sometimes they just seem to disappear. How's the shooter?''

Andrews snorted. "Hangin' in there. The docs still won't let me talk to him. No ID on him yet. It's driving me crazy. I call the nurses twice a day, but they're getting downright irritated with me. They may do him in just so I'll stop calling." He paused. "Which, now that I think of it, wouldn't bother me one damn bit."

Grady understood what the man meant: no officer accepted the death of another one lightly. In fact, most of them took it very personally.

"Stay in touch," Grady said.

"You, too."

He put down the phone then picked it right back up and dialed the medical examiner's office. In a building separate from headquarters, the Harris County Medical Examiner's Office stayed busy all the time. In addition to handling all the metro cases, the pathologists performed contract work for some of the nearby smaller counties that had only justices of the peace for coroners.

"Where do we stand on the Rowling case?''

Grady didn't bother with preliminaries. The secretary who answered the phone knew who he was.

"The autopsy's been done, Lt. Wilson, but we're still waiting on some last-minute reports. We getting to it," she said patiently. "I'm afraid your case isn't the only one we're dealing with right now."

"Of course." He'd heard that before. "How much longer?"

"At least another day. Maybe two or three?"

She sounded so unsure, Grady labeled her reply as a guess more than an answer. He hung up, his frustration only growing.

Becoming restless, he rose from behind his desk a few minutes later. Until he had these last few components—the autopsy report and its subsequent findings—Risa's case would be on hold. And she'd be behind a desk, her life in limbo.

He stopped beside his window and put his hands on the glass, the sun warming his fingertips. When she'd said his name the other day, he'd felt himself falling into a very deep well. He'd been there before with other women. It was a great place to be at first, then something inevitably happened and the walls began to press in.

When that time came—and it always did—it was a long climb out. And he was too damn old to take on something so daunting, especially with someone as young as Risa.

Turning away from the view, Grady went out to the hallway and began to wander aimlessly, his mind on the case. He got coffee, drank half of it, then threw away the cup, pouring another one five minutes later. He stared out the windows in every direction then made the circuit, returning to his office. Sitting down in his chair, he popped up again and walked back into the corridor.

When he found himself outside Risa's cubicle, he wasn't too surprised.

EVEN MORE UNEASY NOW than she had been before she talked to Grady, Risa gave in to temptation Friday morning. She picked up the phone and dialed Catherine's office. But when her assistant answered and said, "Hello," Risa lost her nerve and hung up.

Immediately she picked up the phone and dialed again.

"Lucy? It's Risa. Can you talk?"

In the millisecond of silence that followed her question, Risa suddenly—and unaccountably—felt uneasy. Lucy's unit was always incredibly busy. Sometimes she simply didn't have the time to chat and she'd say so. But this pause felt different.

"I'm trying to decide if I should call Catherine or not," Risa said to fill the emptiness. "Do you think I should?"

"I'm sorry, Risa, but this isn't a good time."

Lucy's voice was cool and remote. "But I wouldn't know how to advise you on that, regardless."

"Oh... Well, okay. I—I'm sorry I bothered you." Risa hung up, confusion and doubt sweeping over her.

She tried Abby next, but once she started talking and making sympathetic noises, Risa couldn't get away fast enough. Pity wasn't what she needed. She said a hasty goodbye and left Abby in midsentence.

Telling herself she was acting crazy, Risa stood up and left her office for the break room down the hall. Maybe some caffeine would clear her mind of the unpleasant thoughts that were beginning to form. As she drew even with the elevators, the doors opened and a woman stepped out from the crowd.

"Crista!"

Risa's cry was automatic. She started forward then suddenly faltered when she realized her friend didn't look as pleased to see her as she was to see her.

Turning, Crista spoke to a man who'd gotten off the elevator with her. "I'll be right there," she said. "You go on."

He shot an unpleasant look at Risa then nodded and went to the end of the hall to wait.

Crista stepped forward. "Risa... How are things going? I, uh, haven't seen you in a while."

"I'm hanging in there," she replied tentatively. "But I haven't really talked to anyone since we went to Luke's service. Is everything okay?'' The question sounded feeble, but Risa didn't know what else to ask.

"I guess we've all been really busy." Crista's expression shifted, and she moved the folders she held from one arm to the other. "I'm sorry I haven't called, Risa, but…" Her voice died out and she looked toward the man who waited for her. "I…I haven't had the time. Things have been kinda rough lately."

Kinda rough? Risa almost laughed. She didn't know what Crista was talking about, but unless she was under investigation for the murder of a fellow officer, too, Risa wasn't impressed.

"Look, I've got to go." Crista tilted her head toward the end of the hall. "I'm sorry but—"

"It's okay. You go on. I understand," Risa said, although she didn't.

Crista nodded, then hurried down the hallway. At the corner, she paused and glanced back and her gaze locked on Risa's. Still standing by the elevator, Risa held her stare. A second later, Crista disappeared.

Risa forgot about her coffee and decided to return to her office. Lost in thought over the strange behavior of Lucy and now Crista, too, Risa didn't look up until she was halfway down the hall. When she finally did, her heart began to hammer.

Grady Wilson stood outside her door.

He was dressed as elegantly as he had been the first time she'd seen him, his dark charcoal suit obviously custom-made...and obviously expensive. Whoever his tailor was, the man knew his business— the cut of the jacket emphasized Grady's already broad shoulders and the pants hugged his narrow hips in all the right places. His tie and shirt matched and were the same color—a soft, seductive gray. A much warmer, much nicer shade than the eyes behind his glasses.

Reluctantly she headed toward him and when she reached his side he greeted her. He was a soft-spoken man, she realized, and in different circumstances, she might have been tempted to label his voice seductive. Right now—as crazy as it seemed—he actually sounded sympathetic when he spoke her name, which made even less sense.

She told herself she was losing it.

Big time.

GRADY GAVE NO INDICATION he'd heard the conversation between Risa and the other woman, but it was clear to him she'd been snubbed. Looking into her dark eyes, he decided she knew *what* had happened but she didn't understand why. Her expression was filled with a confused bewilderment that made him hurt for her. He suddenly wanted to take her into his arms and comfort her. The thought shocked him so thoroughly he physically shook his head as if to dislodge it.

"I was just passing through and I thought I'd stop by." He spoke as she halted beside him, the lie as good as any. "I had to come down and see a guy around the corner. How're things going?"

She nodded, her expression becoming more composed, her professional mask back in place. "Fine," she answered. "Just fine."

He doubted that.

"As you can see, I have plenty of work." She waved a hand toward the files stacked on the desk inside the cubicle. "Our unit secretary is delighted to have some help, but she doesn't yet know how inept I am at filing."

"We all have our strengths and our weaknesses."

Her eyes suddenly sparked and she moved closer to him. For a moment, he thought she was going to take his arm, but she didn't.

"We do," she said, suddenly intense. "And sitting at a damn desk isn't mine. Get me out of here, Grady. I'm going nuts."

"I can't do that. Until the investigation is complete—"

She shook her head impatiently. His spiel meant nothing to her. "But I could help. We'll never get more media coverage than we're getting right now and we should be using everyone we've got. If we don't push hard and ID those guys while the cameras are running, it might take months to figure out who they are.''

She continued to plead her case. She was eloquent—too eloquent—and he felt himself wanting to help her, which he couldn't. He cut her off with his hand.

"Everything you're saying is correct, Risa. But I can't change the rules. You have to be patient and let me do my job.''

She glared at him.

He found himself apologizing then he walked away.

His physical escape turned out to be meaningless, however. Her angry eyes stayed with him the rest of the day.

At five, he left the office and headed for the south side of town and the university. Midway through his lecture, he decided it sounded incredibly stupid. When he counted three kids in the back row snoring, he finally gave up. The sleeping thing didn't usually happen until they were much further into the summer session. He wanted to blame the students, but he knew the fault lay with him. His heart wasn't in explaining Frankl's theory of personality regarding the freedom of the will versus reductionism. He woke everyone up and dismissed them.

Putting the top down on the Porsche, he left the

university and drove faster than he should have up
the Gulf Freeway to the Loop, the humid night air
sticky and hot despite his speed. He was on the Strip
in twenty minutes and not quite sure why—the car
had seemed to find its way on its own. Things frequently happened to Grady that he couldn't explain.

A line of vehicles waited to get into the parking
lot at Tequila Jack's and it was only nine. Apparently
Luke Rowling's death hadn't slowed things at the
club.

Instead of fighting the crowd, Grady turned right
and pulled the Boxster into the darkened lot of a
small office building across the street. Removing his
Official Police Vehicle sign from under his seat and
sticking it on his dash, he decided Dr. Evertt Heim-
len, Dermatologist, wouldn't mind if Grady took up
one of his patient's spots. He wouldn't be lancing
any boils this late in the day.

Sitting back, Grady stared at the steady stream of
patrons and wondered what in the hell he was doing.
Two seconds later, he had his answer.

On the other side of the street, Risa came around
the corner, paused, then entered the bar.

SHE HADN'T WANTED to meet Sun at Tequila Jack's,
but the teenager had insisted. As Risa passed the spot
where Luke's body had lain, she started to tremble,
her eyes jerking to the sidewalk without her permis-

sion. A faint stain still darkened the concrete. Or did it? Maybe she was imagining things again. Crazy things. She'd begun doing that yesterday after she'd talked to everyone. Maybe her friends weren't really her friends after all and maybe Grady really was on her side.

By the end of the day, she'd decided she had to concentrate on what she knew. She made a vow to take her life back and then she'd figured how to do so. Her first step had been to track down Sun.

Tunneling through the crowd now, Risa made her way to the bar stool where she'd sat before. A different bartender brought her a lukewarm Coke, but it tasted even worse than the iced tea she had ordered before and she pushed it away after one sip.

The hooker said she'd already told Grady everything she knew about the shooters, but Risa had told her she needed to hear the story, too. Making up a wild tale connecting the bum who beat up prostitutes with Luke's murder, she'd gotten a promise from Sun to meet her again.

Risa imagined how Grady's gray eyes would look if he found out she'd called the teenager. Quickly eliminating the image from her mind, she told herself it didn't matter. One, he'd never find out and two, if he did, she didn't really give a damn.

"Is this seat taken?"

Risa jerked her head up, her heart jumping into

the middle of her throat as shock, pure and cold, washed over her. How in the hell had he found her?

"No...no," she sputtered. "It's free."

Grady had leaned down so she could hear him, the music as loud tonight as it'd been the night of Luke's death. "Are you sure?" His breath brushed her ear. "I thought you might be waiting for someone."

"Who would I be waiting for?"

His eyes still connected with hers, he tilted his head behind him. "I assumed it might be her."

With a sinking feeling, Risa looked past Grady's shoulder. Sun stood at the other end of the bar and, as Risa watched, she raised her right hand and wiggled her fingers, pointing to a drink in her other hand and mouthing the word *thanks*.

"I bought her a glass of iced tea." Shaking his head, he sat down beside Risa then swiveled the bar stool, his back to the mirror, his face to the crowd. "Strangely enough, that's what she said she wanted."

Risa made no move to answer; she still couldn't believe he was there.

Propping an elbow on the bar, he leaned closer. "What are you doing, Risa?" He smelled of an expensive cologne whose name she couldn't dredge from a suddenly blank mind. "Why did you ask Sun to meet you here?"

"I wanted to talk to her about the case I was investigating when Luke got shot."

"Really? That's not what she told me. She said you wanted to discuss the shooting."

"Does it matter?"

"Actually, yes, it matters greatly." He pulled back and looked at her. She dropped her focus to his mouth—it seemed safer to look at than his eyes. Until she focused. He had full, lush lips and in a bizarre flash she could attribute only to stress, Risa let herself imagine what they might feel like pressed to her throat.

His voice broke her fantasy. "You aren't supposed to be investigating anything," he said. "You're on desk duty."

"I'm on my own free time."

"Cops like you don't have free time."

"You don't know what kind of cop I am. You don't know me, period."

He waited for a heartbeat to pass before he spoke slowly. "Your mother left the family when you were barely two, and you seldom hear from her. You and your three older brothers attended school a block from where you lived. Your brothers are all in law enforcement and your dad retired two years ago from the force. Your father was against you becoming a cop and your brothers agreed because he rules the roost and they agree with everything he says. Regardless of that, right after college, you went directly into the Academy where you graduated top of your class. You spent a year on probation and eighteen months in patrol, then you joined Sex Crimes. You've never been married, you live alone and you're a size six.''

She corrected him without thinking. ''I'm a size eight.''

''Maybe that's what you wear, but you *are* a size six. Trust me on that one.''

She stared at him.

''My ex-wife was a purchaser for Neiman-Marcus. I used to go with her on buying trips,'' he explained. ''I know my Versaces from my Laurens, but the rest of it came from your file.''

Risa made a mental note of the word *ex*-wife. ''All that stuff might be true, but it doesn't mean you know me any better than I know you.''

''Well, what would you like me to tell you?'' He held out his hands in a gesture of openness. ''Ask away. You already know the only secret I tend to keep.''

At his invitation, Risa realized a thousand questions about Grady had plagued her since he'd walked into her house, but she wasn't about to ask him any of them. ''Your personal life is none of my concern,'' she said stiffly.

He shrugged. "Fine by me, but let me point out one thing that *is* your concern."

Risa stood, anxious to get to Sun and even more anxious to get away from him. Looking over his shoulder, she tried to spot the hooker but the corner where she'd stood was now empty. Had he paid Sun to leave? Cursing under her breath, Risa turned back to Grady. "What is that?"

"You have no business doing what you're doing and if you persist, I *will* have your badge pulled."

His threat froze her in place. "Are you serious?"

"Dead serious," he said. "No pun intended."

Recovering quickly, she slung her purse over her shoulder and spoke with renewed determination. "Melinda Rowling is spreading gossip and vicious rumors about me. Since I have no one else to depend on, I'm going to do what I think is best. That means defending myself and establishing the truth. I'll talk to whomever I please."

She started past Grady, but he reached out and stopped her. His grip was loose, his expression casual, yet something told her both could change in a single second.

"Let's not make this harder than it has to be, Risa." His voice was almost pleasant. "Believe it or not, I want the truth and that means I'm on your side."

Deep inside her, a tiny flame of hope flickered.

But being who she was, Risa extinguished the light before it could grow any brighter. What was wrong with her? Was she so desperate for help she thought Grady might be it? He was IA, for God's sake. She could accept that she might be attracted to him physically, but she couldn't trust him. What would it take for her to realize that?

"I'd like to believe you," she said finally, "but I'm afraid I know better." She tightened her grip on her purse. "I know I'm on my own. Don't try and make me think otherwise."

CHAPTER SEVEN

RISA SPENT the weekend trying to reach Sun again. The activity was probably pointless—Grady had obviously convinced the girl to disappear—but she had to do something. The minute her mind went idle, she started thinking about Luke, her friends, or Grady, none of which were subjects she really wanted to examine any closer.

By Sunday evening Risa was almost grateful for her pending family dinner. Normally she dreaded the once-a-month get-together, but driving down South Braeswood to her father's home, she knew the meal would at least give her mind a respite from her problem, even if it wouldn't be a pleasant one.

The smell of burning charcoal greeted her as she stepped out of her Toyota. Her father had turned himself into a fairly decent cook after she'd left home, but he still preferred to grill and in the summer, that's all he did. A glance down the street told her her oldest brother, Ed, Jr., and her middle brother, Phil, had already arrived. As she started up the sidewalk,

Dan, the youngest one, pulled up to the curb and parked.

Pausing between the azalea bushes that lined the walkway, Risa waited as he went around his car and opened the passenger-side door. He'd brought Christina with him. She was in line to be Wife No. Three. If she had half a brain, she would have run for her life, but that apparently wasn't the case, because she and Dan had been dating for two years. He was presently divorcing from Wife No. Two.

The three of them, along with the dog Christina never left at home, started for the front door. As they drew near, Ed, Jr., opened it and waited on the threshold. He shook his brother's hand, kissed Christina, then nodded coldly at Risa, his dark eyes mirrors to her own.

His snub didn't bother her. He didn't have half a brain, either. Unlike Christina, however, he didn't need one—he had his father to do all his thinking. Case in point had been Risa's decision to go into law enforcement. Her father had been against her choice from the very start and Ed, Jr., had agreed completely. Phil, a Harris County sheriff's deputy, had quickly followed suit. Dan was a Department of Public Safety officer. He hadn't been quite as vocal in his disapproval, but his position had eventually lined up with theirs. Women didn't belong in law enforcement. They weren't physically fit for it, they weren't

big enough and they couldn't provide adequate
backup. The only thing her brothers hadn't said was
that women weren't mean enough, but after all the
ones they'd been through, they probably knew that
wasn't true. Phil and Ed were both single at the moment.

They managed to finish most of the meal before
the subject came up.

"My partner's breaking my balls over you, Risa."
Ed, Jr., an HPD cop in the Auto Theft Unit, pushed
aside his plate and glared at her. "When in the hell
is this mess gonna be over? I'm not real crazy about
having my name dragged around in the mud with
yours."

Before she could answer, Phil jumped in. "My
lieu's asked me about it, too. In fact, everybody's
talking about it."

"Thanks for the sympathy, guys," she said. "It's
nice to have the support."

"Hey, you're the one who wanted to be a cop—"

Dan interrupted Ed, Jr. before he could get too
wound up. "Who's handling the case?"

"Grady Wilson." Risa's father answered for her,
his eyes on the steak that covered half his plate.

Risa looked at her dad in surprise. For some reason, she'd never thought of asking him about Grady.
"You know him?"

"I've heard he's a loose cannon," Phil replied.

Risa jerked her eyes to her brother. "I didn't ask you—"

"He *is* a loose cannon," her father interrupted. "Doesn't follow the rules, does things his own way." He sawed a piece off the steak then looked up at her. "He's straight, though," he said grudgingly.

Risa had no doubts about Grady's sexual orientation, but even if she had, she knew that wasn't what her father meant. He was saying Grady was honest.

"That's not what I heard," Ed, Jr., said.

Everyone at the table stared at him.

"Look at his clothes," he said. "Hell, look at his car. The man has too much money for a cop. Everybody knows he's on the take."

"Actually he teaches two night classes at the University of Houston. Maybe his money comes from there." Christina was a secretary for the union head and she knew every cop in HPD, including the ones not in the union. She reached for her beer. "I think he's cute."

As Dan glared at his fiancée, Risa's father spoke again. "Grady isn't who you need to worry about." He caught Risa's eye, his gaze as dark as his scowl. "Rowling's widow is the one you'd better take care of. She's told the whole damn world you were screwing her husband."

Risa steeled herself as the others fell silent. She'd

been waiting for someone to bring Melinda up—she should have known it would be her father.

"Go ahead and repeat the rest of it, Dad," she said quietly. "She's telling everyone I shot him, too. You might as well say it."

For the briefest of moments, she thought her father had winced, but Risa knew better. He had no sympathy for her. As far as he was concerned, she'd made her bed and now it was time for her to lie down in it.

"I don't need to say it," he answered brusquely. "You just did...so the question is, how are you gonna handle her?"

"I'm not sure." Risa cocked her head, her anger and defensiveness getting the better of her, as they always did around her father. "Do you have a suggestion? Maybe you could give me the name of a hit man? Or...since I killed Luke, I guess I could just 'handle' her myself, couldn't I?"

Risa instantly regretted her rash words, but she couldn't bring them back. Everyone around the table froze. She'd actually managed to shock them.

Her father recovered first. Tossing his napkin to his plate, he got up and glared down at her. "You're the one who got yourself in this fix, Risa. You're gonna have to be the one who gets yourself out."

Without a word, Ed, Jr., and Phil stood as well, following her father from the table to the backyard for the cigars they usually lit. Dan sent Risa a look that held a modicum of pity, then he left, too. Seemingly oblivious to the tension, Christina began to chatter as she collected the dirty plates, her schnauzer yapping at her feet hoping for a handout. "I brought a chocolate cake for dessert and we have some ice cream, too. It's really good. I tried a new brand last week and it's sooo rich. I'll get us some." She continued to talk as she disappeared into the kitchen.

Risa left before she came back.

RISA ENDED UP back at her town house without any memory of having driven there. Climbing from her Toyota, cold with anger, she went up the sidewalk, unlocked the house and walked inside, punching in the code to turn off her alarm. The day had gone as badly as she'd known it would. The thought briefly crossed her mind that her prediction of how it would unfold might be seen by some as a self-fulfilling prophecy but she didn't believe so. It'd simply been another round at the Taylors'. *Ding, ding, ding, let the fight begin.*

If *she* had half a brain, she would have stayed away.

Guilt immediately kicked in. Showing up for dinner once a month was all her father expected from her. Regardless of how she felt, he was still her father, and as such, she'd always believed she owed him something.

But maybe she didn't.

Discarding her purse and keys, as well as her thoughts, Risa climbed the stairs and peeled off her clothes as she went. By the time she reached the bathroom, she was naked. She turned on the shower and stepped into the stream of water without waiting for it to warm, her mind focusing on a single topic.

Since the night Luke had died, only one person had seemed to be on her side.

Risa said his name out loud, rivulets of water dripping off her hair and sliding down her bare skin to tap onto the tile. "Grady." Within the shower's walls, the sound of her voice echoed and she wondered how an IA cop, a man she hardly knew, could be the lone individual who seemed sympathetic to her plight. Turning off the water, she leaned her head against the nearest wall and repeated his name, the feel of it lingering on her tongue.

The word was still resonating when something downstairs shattered.

Risa caught her breath, her blood turning as icy as the water had been moments before. What the hell...? The noise had sounded like breaking glass.

Being the cop she was, she instantly started going through her checklist. Had she left the door unlocked? Had she turned on the alarm before she'd come upstairs? Had she opened a window? She couldn't remember. All she could think about was her .44. It was locked up, somewhere deep within headquarters. Her backup weapon, a Glock .35, was in the drawer beside her bed.

Risa stepped from the shower to the bath mat. Soaking wet, she listened closely but heard nothing. Cops were usually paranoid, but as a woman living alone, Risa was worse than most. She kept a weapon of some sort in almost every room. Grabbing the putter she had hidden in the linen closet, she wrapped herself in a towel then moved toward the door. The hinges creaked like a coffin's, but she'd left it open. As she slipped out into the hall, she held her breath and listened again, the golf club gripped with both hands. Once again, there was only silence.

She eased into her bedroom, but the room was empty. If someone had broken into the house, he hadn't made it this far. Going to her bedside, she opened the drawer in the nightstand and felt inside for her weapon, her eyes never leaving the doorway. A second later, her fingers brushed the textured grip of the automatic. She brought the gun out slowly and a minute later she stood at the head of the stairs.

She started down, stopping to listen after each step. By the time she reached the bottom, she'd almost convinced herself she was alone. The house didn't feel as if anyone else was in it, but pausing on the last tread, she didn't let down her guard. Gun held in a double grip, she swept the kitchen first, her eyes searching the corners and shadows. Everything looked okay.

Turning to her right, she slowly entered the living room, her every nerve on alert. Immediately—before she could even fully register what it was—a fluttering motion caught her peripheral vision.

She pivoted, raised her weapon and aimed, her finger on the trigger as she took a shooter's stance. Instead of firing, though, she stared.

Her living-room window had a huge hole in the center of the glass.

Through the gap, a humid summer breeze lifted the blind then released it. With each exhalation, the bottom slat scraped over broken bits of glass on the sill.

Turning, Risa studied the rest of the room. Everything else looked untouched and her chest eased slightly. She took a careful step toward the sofa then found herself paralyzed.

A brick lay on the couch, perfectly centered, perfectly placed. If she'd asked someone to gently arrange it on the cushion, they couldn't have done a better job.

A message had been scratched on one side, and she whispered the words out loud.

"*'Quit now, cop-killer, or die yourself!'*"

GRADY COOKED when he needed to think. At the moment, he had four pots on the stove and the oven preheating. As he reached for his knife, the microwave beeped, too.

He'd barely been home an hour when the M.E. had called him. They'd finished the preliminary report on Rowling over the weekend and the doc had wanted to give the information to Grady as soon as he could.

Actually, that wasn't quite correct. The medical examiner had wanted to *warn* Grady about the results as soon as he could. There was going to be fallout and, in fact, Grady himself was already feeling the effects. The M.E.'s news had taken him by complete surprise, so much so, he'd already begun to wonder if it was past time for him to retire. "Gullible" wasn't a good trait for an IA cop.

The more he thought about what the examiner had told him though, the more he'd begun to wonder, technology be damned. Where was the motivation? When someone killed, there was always a reason, and he had yet to find one where the evidence was pointing.

As Grady chopped onions and tried to puzzle out the news, the scanner on the kitchen counter came awake. He never silenced the thing—the confusing chatter had provided background music to his life for years and generally it was simply white noise. This transmission caught his attention, though.

"Unit Z105, 10-25 at 20V, 1667 Louisa Lane, possible 10-70."

It took him a second to realize why he'd tuned into the call. Louisa Lane was Risa's street. He made the rest of the translation without thinking.

"Meet the woman at this private home. Possible prowler…"

"Unit Z105 to Dispatch, 10-17 to Louisa Lane."

Grady dropped his knife on the cutting board, ripped away his apron and turned to the range, switching off everything with a sweep of his hand. He then ran for the back door, only slowing long enough to grab his service revolver from the closet. He backed out the Porsche with squealing tires and the engine roaring, barely missing the garage door as it lifted.

He beat the cop to her town home.

Wheeling into Risa's driveway, Grady immediately spotted the broken window and imagined a thousand scenarios, all of them bad. When Risa answered the door, he realized he'd been holding his breath, too.

Her dark eyes widened. Clearly she'd expected a uniform—not him. "Grady! What are you doing here?"

"I heard the call on the scanner." His gaze

skimmed her face. She looked upset and exhausted, but he still found himself more attracted to her than he had been to any woman in years. Dressed in jeans and a T-shirt, with wet hair and no makeup, she was gorgeous.

She stepped to one side. "Come on in. Since you're here, you might as well see the damage first-hand."

He followed her into the living room, where she pointed to the sofa. A brick sat in the center, crooked words scrawled across its pitted surface.

Grady read the message. "'Quit now, cop-killer, or die yourself!'"

"Nice, huh?" She spoke lightly but when she raised her eyes to his, he read the anxiousness in her gaze. Despite his latest news, Grady suddenly wanted to strangle the son of a bitch who'd pulled this child-ish prank.

"I was taking a shower and I heard glass breaking. I got my Glock and came downstairs. It was lying there just like that."

"No cars? No sign of anyone?"

She shook her head. "Nothing. They must have tossed it and run. I'm pretty sure—"

The doorbell interrupted whatever she'd been about to say. Trailing the scent of honeysuckle, she strode to the entry and opened the door to a patrol officer. His demeanor businesslike, the cop greeted them both then whipped out a small pad of paper and began to take notes. If he knew about Risa's situation, he didn't say anything about it. When she finished her explanation of what had happened, he stomped around the yard, returned to bag the brick, then promised to file a report. Standing side by side in the living room, they watched him leave fifteen minutes after he'd arrived.

Risa folded her arms and spoke dryly. "I'm sure he'll be right on top of this. No doubt about it."

"Absolutely," Grady replied. "We can all sleep well tonight knowing officers like that are protecting us."

For the first time since he'd met her, Risa smiled at Grady. It was a lopsided expression and more ironic than sincere, but it made his heart thump all the same.

Unnerved by his reaction, he spoke softly. "Are you okay? This must have been upsetting."

She walked to the sofa and sat down, avoiding the place where the brick had been as if it were still there. "It was…unexpected, but I'm more worried about the sentiment than I am the incident." A vulnerability darkened her expression and her voice sounded hesitant when she spoke again. "Grady, please tell me people don't really think I killed Luke. The idea is so outrageous I can't even begin to defend it." She shook her head. "Why would I even *want* to kill him? He was my partner, for God's sake.''

Grady wanted to sit beside her on the sofa, but he wouldn't let himself. The information on the M.E.'s report buzzed inside his head like a hive of angry bees as he perched on the edge of the coffee table in front of her. ''People think you killed him because his wife is telling the world you did.''

''But she's crazy—''

''That may be the case, still Luke never denied having an affair with you, either.''

''I know that,'' she answered quickly. ''But I never slept with him and frankly—''

She broke off with such abruptness that Grady leaned forward, his brain on full alert. ''Frankly, what?''

''I guess I was just relieved all he wanted *was* to take credit.'' She spoke as if she were confessing a weakness and, suddenly, Grady got a glimpse of the cop she really was, the one he'd assumed she was but hadn't seen before now. Dedicated, smart, out to do her job no matter what that entailed, including working with guys who still thought women's lib was a radical idea.

''As long as I didn't have to put up with anything more, I let it slide.''

''How did you know that's all he wanted? He might have been working you somehow...''

"Luke Rowling never put the moves on me," she said with conviction. "Maybe he did on some of the other women officers or secretaries—they thought he was handsome and plenty of them would have been happy to accommodate him—but I wasn't interested, and I made that clear at the very beginning." She paused, as if reluctant to go on. "But it was more than that, though…"

"What do you mean?"

"When a man means business, a woman can tell."

Grady waited.

"It's hard to explain."

"Try."

She licked her lips. "There's a certain kind of tack their interactions seem to take."

Grady could have been fantasizing—he was good at that—but it seemed to him as if something personal passed between them. Something hot. Something dangerous. Something tempting.

"And your relationship with Luke didn't take that route?" he forced himself to ask.

"No," she said. "It didn't even head in that general vicinity—"

"For you," Grady interjected.

"For both of us," she countered. "Like I said before, one, he was married. And two, he was a cop." She shook her head. "I worked too hard and too long to get my assignment in Sex Crimes and I wasn't about to jeopardize all I'd accomplished. There were men in the department, a guy named David Kinner in particular, who was angry about my placement. He was at Melinda's the other day—manning the door, as a matter of fact. I didn't want to give him—or anyone else—something to talk about. Regardless of all that, though, Luke simply wasn't interested in me. I guess I wasn't his type.''

Grady didn't know what to say, mainly because he couldn't imagine a man feeling that way. She misinterpreted his pause.

''You think I'm lying.'' Her voice was flat and devoid of emotion.

Grady stood and walked to the broken window, confused and concerned. He could tell her about the report and let her try and defend herself or he could stay quiet and see what happened. Either way he wouldn't be following the book. That had never bothered him before and it certainly didn't now but he wanted to be fair, whatever in the hell that meant.

With his back still to Risa, he spoke in a soft voice. ''Actually, I do believe you.''

He heard the sofa creak and, a second later, she stood beside him, so close he could smell her shampoo, so near he could feel her warmth. A gust of humid air rattled the blinds.

''Then what's the problem?'' she asked. ''Why

don't you just close my case and let me go back to work?''

He looked down at her. Since he'd seen her last, she'd had her bandage removed. The thin red line made him wince. The bullet had come so close.

''I can't.''

''Why not?''

''Because the M.E. called me this evening. His report is provisional pending the lab tests, but things have gotten more complicated. I shouldn't be telling you any of this, but I generally ignore regulations I think are stupid. Besides, you're going to find out sooner or later anyway so it hardly matters.''

She frowned, a distinct uneasiness coming over her features. ''What do you mean 'more complicated'?''

''Luke was hit with a bullet from a .44,'' he said. ''The perps didn't have .44s.''

She understood immediately. All the color left her face and her cheeks turned the shade of old bones. She swallowed hard. ''That caliber ammo can be used in lots of different weapons.''

''You're absolutely right,'' Grady agreed. ''But the slug that was removed from the body didn't come from just any weapon.'' He put a hand on each of her shoulders as if to steady her. ''It came from yours, Risa. Whether you meant to or not, you shot Luke and there's no getting around it.''

CHAPTER EIGHT

AS HER BRAIN processed his words, the floor dropped out from beneath Risa's feet and her stomach quickly followed. An awful taste filled her mouth and suddenly she wanted to throw up. She forced herself past the sensation and stared at Grady in disbelief.

"That's impossible! I didn't hit Luke! I couldn't have!" She wrenched herself away from Grady's grip. "The report's wrong—it's got to be wrong. Tell them to redo tests. The lab must have made a mistake—"

"There was no mistake," he said. "They shot the water twice and each time the results were the same. The lands and grooves matched perfectly."

To match a gun with a slug or even a fragment of one, the techs shot the suspect's weapon into a barrel of water. Fishing out that round, it was compared to the one in question. The barrel of every gun had its own particular signature—a fingerprint of sorts. As it traveled down the barrel, the departing bullet was engraved with a series of raised grooves and parallel marks that matched each and every time.

Risa felt as if she'd been the one shot. Grady couldn't possibly be telling her the truth. Another thought flashed inside her head. "But I fired seven times. Seven slugs and seven casings were recovered. I couldn't have—"

"Eight casings were recovered."

"What? That's impossible! Look at my weapon," she cried. "Count what I had left—"

"That was done, Risa, and it all added up. You had a thirteen-round magazine in the .44 and there were five rounds in it when you turned it over to IA. That means you discharged your weapon eight times. Eight casings were picked up, logged and matched to your weapon, along with eight slugs...one of which pierced Luke's heart."

She understood what he was trying to tell her, but it didn't make sense. It *couldn't* make sense.

"You're wrong," she said flatly, regaining control of her voice and of her emotions. "They screwed up when they did the testing. I'm too good a shooter to make a mistake like that."

"Risa..."

Her chest felt as if it were caught in a giant fist. "You know my record at the range. If I'd shot Luke, I would have known." Her voice broke as she said her partner's name, but she caught herself. Swallowing hard, she focused all her energy on Grady. "I did not kill him," she said. "You have to believe me."

"I'm sorry, Risa." His gray eyes took on the color of melting snow. "But tests like this don't lie."

RISA HELD HERSELF stiffly, her shoulders straight, her eyes steady. From the look on her face to the way she stood, Grady knew she was telling him the truth…or at least, what she *thought* was the truth.

"I understand that." Her hands became fists at her sides. "But they're incorrect. I did not shoot my partner. If you want the truth like you said you did, you won't accept this report without more investigation."

Reaching out, Grady violated fifteen different department regs and squeezed her shoulder gently, his gaze never leaving hers. She trembled beneath his touch and he softened his voice without conscious effort.

"Accidents happen, Risa. Even if you shot Luke and that's proved, it doesn't mean you're guilty of murder. Friendly-fire tragedies are a sad fact of life—"

"That is *not* what happened."

"When something like this goes down, things get confused. You might believe you didn't shoot him, but you can't be sure. That's why we test and retest."

"And you can keep at it till the end of time," she

replied. "But I'm telling you right now, I didn't shoot him."

Grady wasn't going to change her mind and neither were the facts.

"All right," he said with a sigh he couldn't stop. "I'll register your protest in the morning with Stan Richards, my captain. He'll take it up the ladder from there. In the meantime, you better find yourself an attorney."

"I don't need one," she said stubbornly.

"That may be what you think but—" He broke off when her expression closed. She wasn't listening.

He turned to leave, then hesitated when the damaged window caught his eye. He tilted his head toward the shattered glass. "Do you need some help covering that?"

"I've got something in the garage—"

"Go get it," he instructed. "It won't take me two minutes, then you'll be set for the night."

He expected a protest, but she headed for the kitchen. He heard a door open and close. A few minutes later, she returned with a rectangle of quarter-inch plywood, a battered hammer and four nails.

The wood fit the window perfectly and he turned to her in surprise, his hand holding it in place.

"The kid across the way likes to play baseball," she explained. "Last summer they had a game going and the ball came right through. His dad measured the window and put that over it until the glass guy could come. I kept it.'' She shrugged. "If he's as bad a baseball player as my brothers were, I figured it would happen again.''

Even though her answer made sense, it was clear she was in shock, the startling information he'd just revealed more than she could handle. Her voice sounded brittle and her expression matched it—she looked as if she might fly into pieces at any moment.

Grady wanted to comfort her, to pull her into his arms and pat her on the back and say *It'll be okay,* but he couldn't. That wasn't part of his job description and, in fact, he could get in a lot of trouble for even trying. Definitely with his boss—and probably with Risa.

He put three nails on the windowsill and one between his teeth. "You hold the wood,'' he said from the corner of his mouth, "and I'll hammer it in place.''

She moved closer and leaned over, pressing the plywood against the frame of the window. "There should already be holes where the nails were before.''

He located the first three easily and hammered the nails in. Picking up the last one, he searched the wood trim but couldn't find the original nail hole.

"It's there,'' she said. "It has to be.'' She moved to Grady's left side to get a better line of sight and ended up trapped between him and the window. "I know they're there because I checked earlier. Look closer."

When he didn't answer, she raised her gaze to his.

"I *am* looking." He was staring at her and she stared back. The darkness in her eyes contrasted sharply with her skin, her cheeks so pale her skin seemed made of marble, white and cold. Like a candle on a window ledge, her expression flickered and Grady felt himself pulled relentlessly closer.

He raised a finger and drew it down the line of her jaw.

Her skin was soft and smooth and warm beneath his touch. It didn't feel anything like it looked.

She went so still she had to be holding her breath.

He studied her face. "Your mother must have been a heartbreaker." His voice was a whisper.

"That's not what my father called her."

They were inches apart and, as she spoke, her breath brushed his face. He let his finger drift down to her chin, capturing it between his thumb and forefinger. She looked at him with such intensity he could feel it.

"That's understandable. No man likes to realize his wife is out of love with him. Most of us don't handle the truth very well."

"I hope that's not the case with you."

He spread his fingers on one side of her neck, his

thumb resting on the pulse point of her throat. Drops of water from her wet hair clung to her skin, and he imagined lifting the heavy, dark strands and licking the moisture away from the nape of her neck. The idea was foolish, of course, but he felt as if he already knew the secret spot.

"I'm not afraid of the truth." His eyes fastened on hers. "But sometimes I don't like it."

"Is that how you feel right now?"

She had a full mouth. He wanted to taste it, too. "I don't know what I feel at this point," he lied. "But I have to be sure, one way or the other."

"Then be sure about this." Her voice was hoarse and it scraped along his every nerve. "I didn't shoot Luke Rowling. I don't know why the tests came back the way they did, but I can guarantee you I didn't kill my partner."

Her conviction was so powerful Grady found himself wondering if she carried the same kind of passion into the bedroom. He allowed himself a moment longer to drink in her closeness, then he took a reluctant step back.

Risa blinked and seemed to come to her senses, as well.

Taking the last nail off the sill, Grady pounded it in with one swift hit.

Two minutes later, he was gone.

RISA STARED at the ceiling above her bed and thought.

She thought about dinner at her father's house.

She thought about the brick that had come through her window.

She thought about Grady's mistaken report, and then she thought about Grady himself.

She knew—deep-down-without-a-doubt knew—that she had not shot Luke, but the test results made it hard not to doubt herself. Matching slugs to a particular gun was about as basic as it got.

But she hadn't shot Luke. She *couldn't* have shot him. She would have known.

Wouldn't she?

Tossing the covers aside, she stood with a restless curse. The community had to trust their law-enforcement officials and that meant someone had to police the police. The lecture Catherine had given them at the Academy about that very subject rang in Risa's head. While everyone else in the class had made disparaging remarks about the IA department, Risa had held her tongue. Her father had always said IA had a place and a role to fulfill and she'd absorbed that philosophy, taking it as her own.

But Grady was making a terrible mistake.

She walked to her bedroom window and stared out into the darkness, her thoughts following her. She spent hours at the firing range every month. She liked keeping her skills sharp and she enjoyed the challenge shooting provided her. It was a black-and-white situation with instant feedback. She either hit the target where she aimed or she didn't. Unlike life, the task provided no grounds for argument and the results were obvious.

She leaned her head against the glass, a catch suddenly coming into her throat. If she'd shot Luke... God, she couldn't even imagine how she'd feel were the tests correct. The thought of Luke's son being without a father because of her made Risa's nausea return. Until this point, she had assumed grief and anger over Luke's death had fueled Melinda's accusations and she'd almost understood. As Grady had pointed out earlier, when things like this happened, you had to find someone to blame or you'd go insane over the unfairness of it. But if the tests somehow proved right...

Risa forced her mind still. She couldn't continue along that vein.

Instead, she made herself think about opening the door this evening and finding Grady on the threshold. She'd been shocked to see him, but his expression had surprised her even more. He'd looked...well... almost worried.

Had his reaction been genuine or was he manipulating her?

The first time he'd questioned her she'd learned

how he operated. Quiet, slick and unassuming, he
lulled you into relaxing your guard then pounced.
She'd known this, yet when he'd slipped his hand
behind her hair this evening and drawn her closer,
she'd been unable to resist. In fact, she would have
taken them past that point if he hadn't stepped back.
His chilly eyes had melted her, and his touch had left
her wishing for more. She wanted someone to be on
her side. She needed him to be her friend—or maybe
even something more—and he was too damn smart
not to know that…and use it. He'd only pulled away
because he couldn't yet read her.

But he wasn't her friend.

And she'd better not forget that.

GRADY WAS ALMOST HOME when his cell phone
rang. Because he'd thought of nothing else since he'd
left her house, he assumed it might be Risa and he
answered it immediately. "Wilson here."

"You don't know me," the caller said, "but I got
some info for you. On the Rowling thing."

Normally Grady would have been thrilled at those
words, but disappointment swelled inside him when
he realized Risa wasn't on the other end of the
phone. He pulled himself out of fantasyland and re-
joined real life.

It was The Call.

"Who is this?" he asked automatically.

"You don't care who I am. But you'll want to know what I'm about to say."

He flipped the phone over and looked at the caller ID screen. *Unavailable.* He thought about having the call traced and he stalled as he tried to decide.

"If you've got pertinent information about an on-going investigation, you may be called to testify—"

"Cut the crap, Wilson. It's not your style."

Grady slowed to a reasonable speed, then pulled to the curb. The caller's voice was whiskey rough. Grady had assumed it was a man, but now he wasn't so sure.

"You're right," he said. "So what do you have?"

"This is about Rowling's wife…the nutty one."

"Melinda?"

"Yeah."

"What about her?"

"She's gettin' a little something extra on the side. I thought you oughta know."

Grady leaned back against the car's leather seat, the night suddenly turning even more strange than it had been already. "I don't think I understand."

"Don't be dense. She's been screwing another guy for months and everybody but Rowling knew. I'm surprised you didn't. He was a good cop and so is Taylor. I don't like what that bitch has been spreading around about them now that Luke's gone."

The words and the tone definitely sounded male,

but Grady couldn't be sure. "You mean the gossip about his affair with Risa Taylor?"

"No, I mean the gossip about Taylor popping him." The voice on the other end of the line paused and Grady thought he could hear a dog barking in the background. "If anybody wanted Luke gone, it wouldn't have been Risa Taylor, it woulda been that crazy ass wife of his. *She* was the one sleeping with someone she shouldn't have been. And that's called 'motivation.'"

"Who is he?"

Another long pause came down the line and for half a second, Grady thought he—she?—had hung up. The answer came a second later.

"I don't know his name, but it shouldn't be too hard to find out, even for an IA asshole like you."

Grady gripped the steering wheel tightly, the insult washing over him without impact. He'd been called much worse. "Why is that?"

An ironic twist deepened the caller's voice. "I saw them together and he was wearing the blue. Melinda Rowling's sleeping with another cop."

THE NEXT WEEK DRAGGED BY. Risa tried not to notice, but every day the sideways looks got sharper and the snide remarks got louder. The autopsy results had been leaked and the gossip fires were now blazing.

After an awful weekend, she was grateful when Monday morning came, because it put her a day closer to the monthly luncheon she and her friends had. She'd decided she'd been confused about Lucy and Crista's attitudes because she couldn't face any other possibility. She needed them now. Typically they each called her the day they were to meet and confirmed, and she found herself looking forward just to hearing their voices.

When Risa got to her desk, however, Lucy's message was waiting in the voice-mail box. She'd called late the night before and it struck Risa that her timing had to have been deliberate so she'd miss speaking to her in person.

"I can't make lunch tomorrow," she'd said. "Something's come up. I'll explain later."

The last comment—"I'll explain later"—was Lucy's way of saying, *Don't call me. I'll get in touch with you when I'm ready.*

Risa never quit thinking about her own cases, so she knew nine times out of ten that when Lucy sounded that curt she had the image of a missing child in her mind and she couldn't get it out. But just as there had been when she'd phoned earlier about the gossip, a deeper layer of something echoed in her voice and this time Risa couldn't convince herself to ignore it. She puzzled over what Lucy's problem might be, but before she could take her thoughts further, the phone rang again. This time it was Abby.

"Are we meeting for lunch?"

"Well, I don't know—"

"Because if we are, I can't. I have to work tomorrow and there's no way I can get out of it."

"Okay." Risa nodded thoughtfully. "Work. I understand."

Abby hung up with a promise to call later.

An instant after that, the phone rang again. Risa reached for the receiver as a shadow appeared in her doorway. She answered and glanced up at the same time.

Crista spoke in her ear as Grady captured her gaze. Risa had been pretty successful at telling herself nothing had happened between them Sunday, but seeing him now made her question herself about that situation, too. He held a sheaf of papers in one hand and a coffee cup in the other. Her heart in her throat, she waved the IA officer into her cubicle and tried to concentrate on Crista's voice.

"...only time she had available. I'm really sorry..."

Crista's words finally penetrated Risa's thoughts. "You're canceling, too?" Risa made a sound that should have been a chuckle but was too anxious to be called that. "If I didn't know better, I might think you guys were ganging up on me or something. Just when I need to see you, you're all bailing on me."

"I've been trying to catch this witness for weeks, Risa, and Saturday is the only day she had available. I hope you understand."

"Sure, sure." Risa's eyes connected with Grady's over her desk. "No problem."

Crista's soft goodbye was lost as Risa hung up the phone.

He pushed the papers he'd been carrying across her desk. "More forms," he explained. "You can fill them out whenever you have time."

"Okay."

He made no effort to leave, or to hide the fact he'd listened to her conversation. "Sounds like you're having trouble with your friends."

"It would seem that way." Unbelievably, the phone rang a third time, interrupting her answer. Risa cursed under her breath and refused to even look at the flashing caller ID window.

"You might as well answer it," he said. "You gotta deal with it sooner or later."

Risa glanced at the display, then picked up the receiver and spoke before Mei Lu could say a word. "We're not meeting so don't worry about making up an excuse. Everyone else has already canceled."

A small silence trickled down the line, then Mei

Lu spoke. "That's too bad." she said. "You could probably use the support right now, too."

Mei Lu's answer surprised Risa, but her defenses had already been deployed. "I'm all right," she lied. "Just fine, in fact. But I have a visitor in my office right now. Perhaps we could discuss this another time?"

Risa didn't care how terse she sounded. She was hurting and she'd really needed this get-together, really needed their help. Shouldn't her friends have realized that?

"I'll call back later," Mei Lu said.

"You do that," Risa snapped.

She hung up, replacing the receiver a little too firmly.

In the silence that followed, the mail cart rattled down the corridor then someone called out Debra's name. Grady stared at Risa from the other side of the desk.

"Do you get it now?"

"Get what?"

He nodded toward the telephone. "Your friends are running scared. The last time I dropped by I saw you talking to someone—"

"That was Crista Santiago. Five of us went through the Academy together and Catherine—Chief Tanner—was one of our instructors. We're still pretty close. We meet once a month for lunch."

"Well, Crista was already feeling the heat then. I wondered if you knew they were about to leave you to your own devices."

"We're all very busy and—"

"How many would have made your luncheon this month?"

"Two."

"You and one other?"

She nodded.

"They've heard the rumors." He pulled off his glasses, folded them carefully and dropped them in the inside pocket of his suit. "And know about the report, as well. I'm sure you're aware the results were leaked. Everyone in the building knows the M.E. found your slug."

"Well, the M.E.'s wrong and so are you."

"Which one of your friends told you what Melinda Rowling was saying?" he asked unexpectedly.

"How do you know that's how I found out?"

"Stands to reason."

"It was Lucy. I'm closest to her. But I think it came from—" She caught herself at the very last minute. She'd already told Grady to leave Catherine out of the situation and she needed to do the same.

"From higher up?" he guessed.

She didn't answer. She stared at him instead and, when he seemed to realize she was going to stay quiet, another small smile lifted his lips. "Well, at least you're a loyal pariah. I guess there's something to be said for that.''

"Pariah?'' The word cut. "Is that what I've become?''

"When IA knocks on your front door, anyone with sense goes out the back. Your friends are smart to understand the situation. They have to distance themselves or risk being tarred by the same brush.''

A small, dark wound opened up inside Risa's heart and despite her best intentions to ignore it, she couldn't. Deep down—so far down she hadn't been able to acknowledge it even to herself—she'd been worried about this possibility, especially after thinking over Lucy's attitude and Crista's snub. Each of her friends had worked hard to get where they were and they *couldn't* jeopardize what they'd accomplished.

Grady wasn't telling her anything new, but accepting his words was painful. She had to acknowledge them, though; she couldn't take both sides.

"It isn't fair.'' She spoke quietly, almost to herself more than Grady.

"Doesn't matter. Until things are proved otherwise, you're guilty of something. We just don't know what yet.'' He paused. "And if you're not…well… that'll get buried on page four of the *HPD News*.''

Knowing better, she argued regardless. "But real friends don't act that way.''

He slipped his hand into his pocket and pulled out a silver money clip. Peeling off a dollar bill, he laid it on her desk and stood. "I'm not a betting man," he said, "so this doesn't constitute a wager, but I'm willing to put some money down that says your friends are doing what they have to. They're scared and they can't afford to stand by you. It's the way of the world, Risa." He nodded toward the bill with a cynical expression. "Why don't you put that somewhere for the sake of argument, and we'll revisit the subject when the investigation is over. I might be wrong, who knows?"

Risa reached out, took the money and tucked it into her pocket without a word. With a final look, Grady left her office.

CHAPTER NINE

HER NERVES RAW and scraped, Risa decided after Grady departed her office that she'd simply go home, to hell with Debra's filing. She'd made arrangements to meet the glazier after work anyway so she had an excuse for leaving early. Wheeling out of the parking garage a few minutes later, she headed for the freeway, her mind in a turmoil. Grady's words had made a lot of sense yet the idea of her friends' abandonment was so distressing that Risa actually winced as she thought about it. With a tearful heart, she accepted the fact that he had probably told her the truth, but that didn't mean she had to like it.

The sign for the Hillcroft exit flashed by and glancing at the clock on her dash, Risa abruptly changed lanes. A few minutes after that, she was on South Braeswood in front of her father's home. They hadn't spoken since their disastrous dinner, but that wasn't unusual. She and her family could go for weeks without talking to one another. Pulling to the curb, she parked.

With a greasy rag in his hand, her father answered

the doorbell so quickly he caught her by surprise. The television blared behind him at full volume, his expression uncertain. Suddenly she realized she'd never come home like this before—in the middle of the day, without good reason or invitation.

"I was...down the street," she lied awkwardly, "working on a case. I thought I'd just drop by."

As soon as the words escaped, she cursed silently. Dammit to hell, he knew she was desk-bound. Couldn't she have come up with something better? When he didn't say anything, she started to back up. "Look, if this isn't a good time or something—"

"No, no..." He answered in a gruff voice and held up the oil-stained towel. "It's fine, I just wasn't expectin' anyone. I was working on the lawn mower. Is everything okay?" He stepped aside as he asked his question and Risa walked into the home where she'd grown up.

"No, actually, it's not." She turned. "In fact, nothing's okay."

What she said surprised him and herself, too.

He paused then headed for the rear of the house. "Come out to the garage," he ordered. "I don't wanna lose my place. I got this damn engine spread from here to kingdom come. If I don't get back to it, I'll forget how it goes together."

She was right behind him when he stopped abruptly and looked over his shoulder, his eyes dropping to the wrinkled black skirt and jacket she'd yanked out of her closet this morning. "Oh, wait, you got on a nice suit there, don't you? You don't wanna mess it up and get all dirty. What am I thinking about?"

Risa didn't know what to do. He'd never come that close to complimenting her before and she could hardly believe he'd even noticed.

"No, it's...it's okay, Pop," she stammered, too disconcerted to say anything else. "The garage is fine."

He shrugged and resumed his path through the crowded house. In something of a daze, Risa followed him out the back door. A bundle of gray hair and yapping confusion jumped on her as she cleared the threshold.

"Get down, you useless fleabag!" her father growled. "Get the hell outta here."

"Isn't that—"

"Christina's mutt?" He made a halfway kicking motion toward the dog that had already slunk away at his voice. "Yeah, it's hers, all right. She asked me to take the mangy jackass to the vet this afternoon and I said I would for some ungodly reason I can't remember right now."

Her dad doing Christina a favor? Risa felt as if she'd wandered into a parallel universe. Who are you, she wanted to ask, and what have you done with my father?

He stepped over a pile of engine parts and waved his rag toward a lawn chair. "Have a seat."

Risa did as he instructed, a sharp memory from her childhood coming to her along with the scent of spilled diesel and used oil. For a while, when she'd competed with her brothers for her father's attention, she'd thought she could win if she hung out with him in the garage and acted interested in whatever he was doing. He hadn't seemed to appreciate the company and she'd eventually given up.

Leaning against the fender of his '58 Chevy, he crossed his arms and stared at her. The silence built.

"I'm in deep shit," she said finally.

"I know," he answered.

"The ballistic reports are in. They're saying the slug that—" she stopped and swallowed "—that killed Luke came from my weapon."

He didn't react and she realized he already knew. She wasn't surprised.

"Tell me everything."

She recited the story, Grady's information coming out in halting sentences that she couldn't seem to organize. She kept expecting her father to interrupt and say she wasn't making sense, but he didn't. In fact, he didn't utter a word, even after she finished.

Instead, he stared past where she sat, his eyes going to the empty street in front of his house. She couldn't read his expression because he didn't have one, but suddenly she knew what he was thinking.

He hadn't wanted her to become a cop. He'd made it clear he didn't want her to go to the Academy. He'd practically predicted disaster would follow. And now it had.

Risa wanted to kick herself. What on earth had she been thinking? Why had she come here? Looking to her father for help was as stupid as looking to Grady for sympathy. The stress she'd been under lately had obviously pushed her over the edge.

She stood up so abruptly the lawn chair collapsed behind her with a rattle. Her father jerked his eyes away from the street and stared at her.

"I shouldn't have come here," she said.

"You're right," he said, breaking her heart before he continued. "You should be talking to that IA goon instead of me. For God's sake, he's obviously got his head up his ass or he would have already realized what's going on."

Prepared for something else entirely, she frowned in confusion. "What are you saying?"

He looked at her with an expression that seemed to confirm her earlier assumption. He thought she was an idiot. She wanted to flee the criticism but she couldn't; she had to hear his answer first.

It came quickly and with unmistakable authority.

"Things aren't always what they seem, Risa. You, and apparently Wilson, too, are looking at the surface. You're seeing what they want you to see."

"Who's they?"

"I don't know yet."

His cryptic answer only served to frustrate her more. "Look, Dad, I'm not getting it."

With a heavy sigh, he tossed the oil-stained rag toward a pile of others in the corner. "I had this case...it was November '85. I remembered the date 'cause we were grilling steaks and listening to the Royals and the Cards. It was game six of the Series and just as that asshole ref made his stupid call, we had to leave."

"And?"

"Our lieutenant's brother-in-law had been shot and he wanted us to go down to Brazoria County where the guy had been a sheriff's deputy. We were supposed to find out what the hell had happened, talk to the sheriff, that kind of stuff. The lieu couldn't go 'cause his wife was going ape-shit and he trusted me and Bobby. We left and went to the scene." He paused as if remembering. "Some kids had gone out to this rice field to park and smoke pot and they'd found the body."

Instantly hooked, Risa stared at her father in fascination. He'd shared stories like this with her brothers when they'd been younger, but he'd never included her. At least, not intentionally. She'd always listened from a nearby hidden spot. "What had happened?"

"The sheriff said suicide. Showed us the wound and the pistol, blood everywhere. Situation seemed cut-and-dried and we hauled the body back to Houston. The minute the M.E. peeled back his eyelids, he told us the truth. Somebody had smothered the son of a bitch first. They'd shot him to cover it up and make it look like a suicide."

With her brain spinning, Risa tried to put the pieces together.

"Was it the sheriff?" she asked.

"Of course not. The sheriff woulda known better." He paused. "At least, I hope he would have. No, it was the wife. She couldn't tell a petechial hemorrhage from a hole in the ground, not to mention the fact that her now-dead husband had no residue on his hands. She'd drugged him first and that showed up in the chem analysis, too."

"So she shot him after he was dead? Where'd the blood come from?"

He seemed surprised by the astuteness of her question. "It wasn't his blood—she'd cut up a chicken or something. Hell, the woman wasn't a rocket scientist, okay? She just wanted to fake the suicide, take his money and run." He paused. "If she wasn't bright enough to know insurance won't pay off on suicide, do you think she could have figured out anything else?''

Risa went silent as she considered his words and put the information into context. Finally she spoke. ''Pop, Luke's murder wasn't staged. It happened in front of my eyes.''

''Maybe,'' he said. ''Maybe not.''

''I saw him fall and he stopped breathing right in front of me. I *watched* him die.'' Her voice almost cracked, but she caught herself at the last minute. ''I don't think this is the same thing.''

''Of course it isn't the same thing, Risa, but for God's sake, use your brain. At first glance, a situation can look like one thing, then when you look again, it can appear to be something else entirely different. *That's* my point. Don't settle for the obvious. You can't always believe your eyes—or an autopsy report. Dig deeper.''

''That's good advice, but I have a feeling I can dig to China and I'm still not going to find the truth.''

''Well, you better find it,'' he warned. ''Your life depends on it.''

He was right, of course, but suddenly the situation seemed overwhelming. She'd lost her friends, her career and her partner. The world felt upside down with her father helping her and Grady kissing her. She couldn't think straight, much less creatively.

Behind the garage, Christina's dog barked once

then quickly fell quiet, as if remembering where he was. She spoke quietly. "What happens if I can't?"

"That's not an option. You're a Taylor. And Taylors don't fail."

The connection Risa had felt between them shriveled under the force of his answer. Her throat went tight as he stared sternly at her.

"Pull yourself together," he ordered, "and act like you know that."

RISA WASN'T CONVINCED of her father's argument when she drove away that afternoon. She was equally unsure which had surprised her more—his idea or the fact that they'd actually discussed the situation without one of them getting pissed off and storming away in a huff. He'd hurt her feelings with his gruffness, but she somehow felt better after talking to him, too. It was a weird combination, then again, her life had been nothing but weird since the shooting.

It seemed like a miracle, but the glazier was right on time. As soon as he finished and she'd paid him, Risa changed clothes then grabbed her duffel bag from the closet and left again. Thirty minutes later she parked in front of the private gun range where she practiced. A lot of cops belonged to the club and Risa had been a member for years. The owners were good people. Usually a stickler for doing her own cleaning and maintenance, she'd let the club's tech adjust her trigger pull last month. He'd done a good job.

Regardless of that, she didn't really want to run into anyone she knew. But if she did, well, she did. She had nothing to hide, she told herself. She should act innocent because she was innocent.

Looking neither left nor right, she registered at the front desk, got her lane assignment and walked directly to the indoor shooting area.

The club was high tech all the way with twenty-five air-conditioned, soundproofed lanes. The stations were four, maybe five, feet wide and fifty feet long, each one outfitted with a computer that allowed the shooter to select from over twenty different courses. The programs were preset and tactical, challenging for some, but useless as far as Risa was concerned. They felt like video games to her and she wasn't there to play.

Dropping her duffel to the black rubber mat at her feet, Risa knelt down and pulled out her equipment, including her pistol.

The range had special wall tiles that absorbed the sound as well as bullets, but she always wore ear protection and safety glasses, too. With everything in place, she punched up her program, adjusting the speed and placement to make the task more difficult as she progressed, took her stance and began to fire. An hour later, she was sweating and exhausted, but the tension she'd had in her neck and arms came from physical effort and not from stress and worry.

She flipped on the gun's safety catch and stepped back from her stand, her eyes briefly meeting the curious gaze of the man in the lane next to her. She knew him, but from where? A second passed then she placed him, a hard knot forming in her chest.

He was the blonde who'd been at Melinda Rowling's side before she'd attacked Risa.

Laying his weapon on the table before him, the cop pulled off his own ear protectors and said hello, sticking his hand out in a friendly manner. "You're Risa Taylor," he said. "Kurt Trundle. We met at—"

"At the Rowling house." Risa preempted him. "I thought you looked familiar."

"I'm surprised you remember. Things got a tad confused that day, didn't they?"

He seemed amicable enough, but Risa no longer trusted her judgment.

"I'm afraid they did." Speaking in a dismissive manner, she decided to cut her session short even though she'd paid for two hours. She squatted beside her bag, put her gun away then her towel and zipped the bag shut. Standing up, she slung it over her shoulder and started to leave.

His voice stopped her before she managed one step.

"Melinda was really upset."

It seemed rude to simply walk away without comment. "I'm sure I would have been upset myself if I'd just lost my husband," she said.

"Maybe so, but losing a partner's no picnic, either. You've had a tough go of it, too." Reaching inside the pocket of his black T-shirt, he removed a card and held it out to her. "If you need a shoulder, I've got a broad one. I'd be happy to listen."

His offer startled her, but she wasn't sure why. Men had been trying to give her their phone numbers—or get hers—since she was twelve. His manner was matter-of-fact, though, and not a come-on. He was being friendly, nothing more.

Wasn't he?

She accepted his card. "Thanks. I'll keep your offer in mind."

"Please do."

She returned his smile and started once more toward the door, the direction taking her between him and the wall. Just as she drew even with him, he reached out and patted her shoulder.

"I mean it." His eyes were bright and blue. Too blue. "Call me."

She muttered something vague then quickly left.

The incident, strange at it was, was forgotten until later that evening when her thoughts returned to the conversation she'd had with her dad. Passing a picture of him and his unit back in its heyday, she paused.

Kurt Trundle didn't look like any of them with his fine blond hair and bright blue eyes, but something about him reminded her of all the old-time cops in the photo. They were masters at saying one thing but meaning another and, even as a kid, she'd sensed their subterfuge and arrogant attitudes of invulnerability. Trundle's assurance mixed with her father's words and her brain started twirling.

Had her father been pulling the same kind of shit his former cronies liked to pull? He'd suggested a setup, then implied the question: Why would *anyone* want Luke dead?

A new idea came into her mind. Rumors of corruption had been floating around the department for years and her dad had to have heard them all, as connected as he was. Maybe he'd wanted her to turn her mind in that direction but he knew better than to push her, because she would have gone the opposite way. Planting a seed and letting it germinate would produce far better results.

She went upstairs but she didn't sleep. In fact, when her phone rang a little past midnight, she was still awake.

Her father's gruff voice answered when she said, "Hello?"

"I been thinking about something since you left,"

he said curtly. "Then I talked it over with Bobby. I think we might be on to something."

Risa was glad she was lying down. She could count the times her father had called her on one hand. She responded slowly, unsure of what he expected of her. "Okay."

"I don't know who 'they' are yet," he said in his raspy voice, "but I think I know what's happenin'."

Risa wondered if she should take his words at face value or try to interpret them. Earlier, she'd been convinced he was manipulating her, yet now she wasn't so sure. He almost sounded excited.

"And that is…" she asked cautiously.

"Somebody's settin' you up," he pronounced unequivocally.

She took the phone away from her ear and stared at it in openmouthed disbelief. Bringing it back, she said, "What? That's crazy…I—I…"

"Never even considered the possibility," he finished flatly.

"Of course not! Because it's too outrageous. Why on earth would anyone want to frame me for Luke's murder? That doesn't make sense."

"But you shooting him does?" He took a breath and she heard the schnauzer barking in the background. "The man's dead and he wasn't hit by a train. The lab says your bullet killed him. Either you shot him or somebody else did. If somebody else did—as 'outrageous' as that sounds to you—they did it in a way that makes you look guilty. Which version do you wanna believe?''

She ignored his question and asked one of her own. ''How'd you come up with this theory?''

''Bobby and I had a case once that was a professional hit, a setup. We can't remember all the details, but we remembered enough to figure out the same thing might be happenin' to you. Bobby's got his second cousin down in records looking up the case so we can get the details back.''

''Dad, I appreciate the help, but this sounds like such a long shot—''

''It may be,'' he conceded, ''but the other option is that you killed him. You like that better?''

''I didn't shoot my partner,'' Risa said quietly.

''Then we better figure out who did,'' he said, ''or you're gonna be the one who goes down for it.''

GRADY TOLD Richards about Risa's complaint on Tuesday morning. ''I'm still waiting on the M.E.'s final report, but she says she didn't shoot him and she's disputing the facts. I can't finish until her complaint is resolved.''

From behind his desk, Grady's boss looked as if he wanted to explode. ''I told you to take care of this case, Wilson. What the hell went wrong?''

"Nothing went wrong." Grady sipped his Starbucks. "She doesn't believe the test results and she wants to contest them."

"Is this woman a cop or what? I can't believe she thinks like this. It's crazy! Any idiot knows those findings can't be dicked with and what's more…"

He continued sputtering until he realized Grady had yet to reply.

"Risa Taylor is an excellent officer with an outstanding record." Grady paused. "Unlike some in the department, she knows what she's doing and she does it well. She deserves a full investigation."

Richards had never been on the street. He'd served his patrol time by driving the mayor around town. From there, he'd gone straight into his first, but not his last, admin position.

Richards's eyes slid past Grady's, then quickly came back. They held defiance at Grady's subtle putdown—after all he *was* Grady's boss—but a certain amount of curiosity was in them, as well. "Then the tests are wrong?"

"I didn't say that," Grady replied. "But I'm working the angle."

"And the brick incident?"

"Too soon for a report, but I doubt we'll get anywhere with it. Somebody's pissed and they wanted to let her know. The brick was thrown the same night

I got the M.E.'s initial report, though. I need to make sure there isn't a link between the two.''

"When will you be done?''

"When I'm finished.''

"I need a time, Wilson. The mayor doesn't like this dragging out and the press is pounding my ass for a resolution. I want to turn this over to the CRC and the assistant chief ASAP.'' He glanced at his fake Rolex that fooled no one then looked back at Grady. "I've got a reporter due any minute and he's gonna want an update.''

Disgusted, Grady stood and drained his coffee, then crushed the cup and tossed it into the wastebasket. "When I have a recommendation, you'll be the first to know.''

He walked out of Richards's office and directly into Risa's path.

She spoke without as much as a hello. "I need to talk to you.''

Distracted and nervous, she looked as if she'd fallen out of bed and come straight to the office. Her dark hair had been combed and she'd put on a little lipstick, but if she'd had on pj's beneath her suit jacket he wouldn't have been too surprised. He marveled at the way this endeared her to him. Before he'd met Risa, the women who'd always caught his eye had looked as if they'd just walked out of the salon and were heading for the mall.

Seeing her in the flesh released the demons Grady
had been fighting since the night at her house. Desire.
Lust. Heat. He thought he'd finally banished them,
but now he knew he'd thought wrong, especially after defending her to Richards. He wondered if she
could tell. Then he wondered if she knew anything
about Luke's wife having an affair.

With Richards's eyes on his back, Grady took
Risa's elbow and steered her out of his boss's line
of sight. "This isn't a good place for you to be."

"I don't care. I need to talk to you," she repeated.
"Right now."

THEY ENDED UP six blocks down the street. Sam
Houston Park was an oasis of green in the middle of
downtown Houston, the towering skyscrapers at odds
with the eclectic assortment of historic structures that
had been moved to the park over the years. Risa led
Grady straight to the one that was her favorite, the
Saint John Church. They entered the dark and
gloomy one-room building. It was cool and quiet and
very empty.

She slid into the nearest pew, its cypress planks
polished over the years by the Lutheran congregation
that had used it since 1891. A plaque informed vis-
itors the Heritage Society had moved the church to
the park from the northwestern part of the county in
1968, but in her mind Risa could still see the stern

German folk who had come here to pray and sing and probably confess.

Grady sat beside her, his arm across the back of the pew. "I'm all yours," he said.

She took a deep breath and met his eyes. They looked less chilling and more intense in the dimness of the old building but she wasn't sure. Her nervousness made her uncertain of everything, including the reason she'd brought him here. The more she'd thought about her father's suggestion, though, the stronger her conviction had grown. She'd woken this morning, knowing she had to tell Grady.

Without giving herself more time to fret, she spoke. "I talked with my father for a long time yesterday and he basically said we aren't looking deep enough. Then he mentioned something I hadn't considered before. After sleeping on it last night, I came up with more questions than answers and I thought, well, I thought I should talk to you about it."

"What did he say?"

"I'll explain in a minute, but first I have to ask you something. It might not make sense to you, but I have to know." She hesitated then took the plunge. "Do you think it's possible that Luke could have been dirty?"

GRADY BLINKED as Risa's words registered. He'd been thinking about how much he'd like to bury his face in the crook of her neck…right below her ear, in that tender spot—

"Grady?" she repeated his name.

"I heard you," he said. "But I don't have an answer I'd swear to at the moment. As far as I know he was clean."

"Well, remember the other night when I told you about David Kinner? He's the guy who was at Melinda's? He wanted the position in Sex Crimes that I got instead…"

"And?"

"When I came into the station this morning, I checked on Kinner. He was off Sunday night." She paused. "His unit secretary told me he was gone because he's building a cabin up by Lake Conroe and he had to brick the facade this weekend."

Grady didn't react, but this time it wasn't because he was thinking about Risa; he was remembering his anonymous caller from the other night. The one who'd said Melinda Rowling was having an affair. With a cop.

"There are construction sites all over Houston, Risa. Anyone could have picked up a brick anywhere and you know it." He spoke blandly.

"I agree," she said, "but you'd have to admit it's mighty coincidental, isn't it?"

"Maybe. But there's no connection—"

"Yes, there is." She moved closer as if to better

make her point. "Luke was an ambitious cop and he hadn't gotten to the top rung in SC without stepping on some toes. I never gave it any thought, but there were some very unsatisfied officers in our unit who believed he had manipulated the system to get where he was, payoffs for advancement, that kind of thing. Kinner was one of them and he hated both of us. He would have gotten a double play by killing Luke then somehow blaming me."

"And 'somehow' covers the fact that Luke was shot with your gun? That you were holding at the time?"

"That's a problem," she conceded, "but I think the idea bears looking into. Everyone's speculated about corruption in the department for years. Luke was a good cop, but it's not inconceivable that if he paid for his promotion…"

"You're stretching it."

"Maybe I am, but this is my career we're talking about." Her dark eyes blazed with sudden determination. "If you won't look into this possibility, then I'll start my own investigation," she warned. "I'll prove you're wrong, all on my own, if I have to."

"Look, we've talked about this before. *I'm* the one who'll work this out." Grady tensed. "Let me handle this."

"I would if you were handling it," she said hotly. "But you're not. You already made up your mind and now you're finding the facts to back it up. Like that bogus report from the lab. I'm not going to let you railroad me.''

She stood up and tried to pass him, but Grady blocked her exit from the pew. They were inches apart in the cool dark and his hands were on her shoulders.

"You've misunderstood me from the beginning," he said.

"I don't think so."

"I've defended you. I've cut you slack. I've told you things about the case you shouldn't know until it's over." He gripped her tightly. "I know you think I'm lying, but this is the truth. I *want* you to be innocent, Risa."

"Why should I believe that?" She searched his face as if she could read the truth from his expression. "What do you care? Why do you want me to be innocent?"

"I want it because you're a good cop and because HPD needs officers like you. I want it because you want it." He paused and leaned closer, breathing in her perfume and her nearness. "But mostly I want it...because I want you, too."

CHAPTER TEN

GRADY'S LIPS CLOSED over Risa's. Because he was so quiet and unassuming, she expected something gentle from him, something soft, but his kiss was nothing like that. It took her by complete surprise, eliminating her hesitations and replacing them with unrelenting desire. It was a lightning strike she didn't expect.

The shock rippled over her yet the power of his kiss didn't dissipate. It seemed to grow instead, taking her energy as its own and fueling her need. Risa held on to Grady's arms and tried not to react, but when his tongue parted her lips and the kiss became more intimate, she relinquished all control, a low groan building in the back of her throat. He matched the sound with one of his own and she felt it as much as she heard it, his body vibrating. They'd both been holding back, she realized belatedly, and now they'd reached the point of explosion together.

She wasn't sure how long the kiss lasted but when he pulled away, she wasn't ready.

''What in the hell am I doing?'' he asked.

"I...I think that's called a kiss."

"I've never had a kiss like that before. Are you sure?"

"Not really." The confession slipped out on its own. "Maybe we should do it again, so we can be positive. I'd hate to not know."

She could tell he liked the idea. He started to bring her closer but stopped and did just the opposite, dropping his arms to take a step backward.

"This is insane. We can't do this. I'm supposed to be investigating you. We could both get thrown off the force, and we'd deserve it for being so stupid."

He was right.

She nodded.

"Trading my job for a woman like you might be worth it to me," he said, "but *you* can do better. A helluva lot better. I'm too old for you. I've seen too much. I work too hard. I'm a cop and you don't date cops."

Their eyes connected in the gloomy church. A second passed and her pulse roared in her ears. Then he pulled her to him and they started all over again.

They never saw the shadow in the window.

GRADY LEFT Risa standing on the sidewalk off Travis Street and headed straight for the parking garage. Her suggestion seemed like a remote possibility, but if

David Kinner had had it in for Risa and Luke *and* he turned out to be Melinda's lover, Grady would have to start over. And he wouldn't even know where to begin because the physical evidence, like an elephant in the living room, would still be too overwhelming to ignore.

Between the construction and the traffic, it took him an hour to get to the Rowling house and he had plenty of time to cuss himself. He'd been crazy to kiss Risa, but how could he have resisted? He savored the memory of their encounter then told himself it'd never happen again. At the very same time, the other side of his brain was plotting how soon he could see her again.

Melinda Rowling answered the doorbell after four rings and Grady almost wished he'd called first. She wore a rumpled, dirty housedress and a very blank look.

"I'm Grady Wilson," he reminded her through the screen door. "I'm with HPD Internal—"

"I know who you are," she interrupted. "What do you want? I'm kinda busy right now."

"I'm sorry," he said in his most sympathetic voice. "But I need to ask you a few more questions. I'm trying to wrap up a loose end or two."

She looked as if she wanted to close the door in his face. Half expecting just that, Grady was surprised when she threw the lock and pushed the door open instead. "C'mon in," she said in a reluctant voice. "I can give you ten minutes."

The day of the memorial service, the home had been neat and clean, but that was no longer the case. Unfolded laundry was piled on the sofa and dirty dishes littered the dining-room table. A thin coat of dust covered everything. She waved him toward a recliner as she pushed aside some of the wash and sat down on the couch. She didn't seem to notice when half of the load tumbled to a rug that looked as if it hadn't been vacuumed in a month.

She threaded her fingers through her dank hair then dropped her hands to her lap. "You're the one who took that woman out of here, aren't you?" Not waiting for his answer, she went on, spitting out the words as if they tasted bitter. "Luke's partner...Risa. She shot him, I know that for a fact."

Her outspokenness should have amazed him, but it didn't. Her dilated eyes and dazed attitude registered, and Grady remembered Risa's earlier comments. Melinda was either drunk or high.

"How do you know that, Mrs. Rowling?"

"I been told."

"By whom?"

"The same person who told me they were sleeping with each other."

"Was that David Kinner?"

She looked at him so emptily he knew the answer before she spoke.

"David who?"

"Kinner. He's a cop—"

"Oh, the guy on Luke's team. No, of course not." Switching gears as abruptly as he had a second before, she said, "She had a thing for him, you know. He did for her, too."

He assumed she was back on Risa. "I'm surprised you'd say that, Mrs. Rowling. Most women wouldn't be as forthright about their husband's affairs."

"She's beau...ti...ful." She pronounced all three syllables so distinctly he knew she was trying not to slur her words. "What kinda man wouldn't wanna sleep with Risa Taylor?"

Grady definitely didn't have an answer for that one. She rambled on.

"We...we'd been married five years and I...I thought..." Her restless fingers found a kitchen towel and she brought it to her face. She touched her eyes with the rough fabric, then let it fall. "We'd had our troubles, just like any married couple, but I thought I could make it work. After the baby came, I...I put on some weight and it was hard, but I thought having a kid would make Luke change."

"Change how?"

She stiffened at his question but answered immediately. "I thought it'd make him want to stay home more."

Her answer made sense, even though her delivery seemed strange. "I understand," Grady said. "You wanted some help. It's hard to find time for yourself when you're a new mom."

"Time for myself?" She looked puzzled. "Why would I want that?"

"Well, I assume you have a job, a career. Most women these days have their own lives beyond the family. Even if you didn't work outside the home, I can see how you might want to get out and be with your friends." Or your lover…

Whatever she'd used to dull her senses was wearing off. Her voice went sharp. "What are you talking about?"

"I'm investigating your husband's death, Mrs. Rowling, but that means I have to look at everything in his life. Even though he's gone, in a sense, I have to get to know him and his family as well."

Her skin took on a greenish tone and, for a moment, he was afraid she might get sick. "I'm sure you already know the important stuff," she said.

"Do I?"

She blinked.

"I've heard some rumors, Mrs. Rowling."

"They aren't true!"

"You don't even know what I was going to say."

"It doesn't matter," she said, her voice going higher. "They aren't true, whatever they are. Everything was fine. Just fine. We were…we were a perfect family."

"Perfect families don't generally include affairs."

She clutched the towel in her lap, wrapping her fingers around it as if she were drowning and it was a rope. "I don't think he loved her, if that's what you're implying."

"I'm not talking about Luke and Officer Taylor," Grady said. "I'm talking about you. I've been told you were seeing someone outside your marriage, Mrs. Rowling. Another officer, in fact. Is that true?"

She jumped up from the couch, her face alarmed. "That's outrageous! Who told you that? You ought to be getting the woman who killed my husband instead of coming over here and harassing me! How dare you barge in here and accuse me of something like that?"

Grady remained seated. "I'm not accusing you of anything, Mrs. Rowling. I'm telling you what I was told and asking if it's true."

"It's not true," she said hotly. "Not at all. It's a lie. Why would I even want to have an affair when I had a husband who looked like Luke?" She pursed her lips then nodded toward the door. "I think it's time for you to leave. Your ten minutes are up."

AFTER RISA WENT BACK to her office, she decided she didn't want to think about what had happened in the park, but her mind didn't seem to care what she wanted. All she could concentrate on was Grady.

Who would have thought he could kiss like that?

Sure, she'd been attracted to him, but she'd attributed her feelings to the desire to have him on her side, not in her bed. Now she wondered. The quiet, bookish exterior hid an unexpected man, his cold gray eyes and piercing demeanor a cover-up for something far different. What else, she wondered, lurked behind his facade?

Realizing she was making a giant mistake but willing to risk it, Risa did the only thing she knew that would get her thoughts off Grady. She picked up the phone and called Mei Lu. She didn't really know what to expect, since she hadn't spoken to any of her friends since the canceled lunch date, but in retrospect, Mei Lu had seemed the least upset of all of them. More importantly, Mei Lu was very well connected, both inside the force and out. All Risa needed was a simple answer to a simple question. Surely she'd help her.

Mei Lu answered on the third ring.

"It's Risa. Have you got a minute to talk?"

Was there a hesitation or not? Risa couldn't tell.

"There's a meeting in half an hour I need to go to, but I've got some time. How are you doing, Risa?"

Was her voice hard? Did she sound aloof?

"I'm fine," Risa said, her own voice as cool as she could make it. "I have something I need to ask you, though."

"What is it?"

This time she was sure she heard caution in Mei Lu's voice. Risa plunged ahead regardless. "I had a brick come through my window the other night and I think David Kinner might have had something to do with it."

"Oh, Risa... That jerk." Mei Lu's distress sounded genuine, but Risa wouldn't let herself believe it was. "I'm so sorry. You weren't hurt, were you?"

"All I suffered was a broken window."

"Well, I've heard nothing," Mei Lu said. "At least not about Kinner—" She stopped all at once, the break in her speech too abrupt for Risa to ignore.

"Because everyone's too busy talking about me?"

The usually unflappable Mei Lu rarely got rattled but she did so now. "Well, actually...yes. Your situation is being discussed a lot right now."

Despite herself, Risa felt her throat tighten. "You don't believe I killed Luke, do you?"

"I don't know what to believe, Risa. The ballistics tests the lab performed—they're awfully reliable, you'd have to admit."

"Oh, they're reliable, all right." Risa spoke in a

voice tinged with bitterness. She was too tired to hide
her emotions, especially with Grady's wager in her
mind. "More reliable than my friends."

"Risa, please—"

"Please what, Mei Lu? No one's called, no one's
come by. Everyone bailed on the luncheon. It's pretty
obvious you guys are abandoning me."

"Maybe we're not helping you as much as we
should, Risa, but—"

"How about you're not helping me at all?" Risa's
anger got the better of her, her frustration bubbling
to the top and boiling over. "I didn't expect anyone
to hold a rally for me on the square downtown, but
I thought I could count on my friends to support
me."

"We're all concerned—"

"That's for sure! You're concerned about your
own positions, aren't you? I'm persona non grata and
so are my problems. Has it occurred to any of you
that I might be innocent?"

"It's occurred to all of us," Mei Lu said quietly.
"But you have to see the position we've been put
in, Risa. If we defend you too vigorously, they'll say
we're just sticking by you because you're a woman.
And God help us all if there was any hint that Catherine might come to your aid. Each of us has to be
very careful, yourself included. We're handling the
situation the best way we know how—and that might

end up being different for each of us. We have all had to take a step back from our friendship." She paused. "Maybe Kinner has a point, albeit a crudely expressed one."

"What do you mean?"

"We're each going to have to use our *own* brains to work this out, Risa. There's no other way."

Silence came down the line because Risa didn't know what to say.

"Suppose our positions were reversed," Mei Lu said softly. "What would you do if you were in our place?"

Her question wasn't a new one. Ever since she and Grady had discussed her friends' reactions, Risa had been thinking about the situation and even though she didn't like what it said about her, she knew that nothing meant more to her than her career—she'd worked too long and too hard to jeopardize it for anyone, especially for herself. The friendship and closeness she'd shared with the five women was great but the preservation of all her efforts was more important.

She might have made the very same choice her friends had, but that knowledge still didn't mitigate the sting of their self-imposed distance.

"I don't know what I'd do," she said finally. "But I pray to God I'll never find out, because right now I wouldn't wish my life on my worst enemy."

She gave Mei Lu no time to comment. She simply said goodbye and hung up the phone. There would be no more pretending now. Friends or not, the break was complete; they were gone and Risa was on her own.

RISA FINALLY MANAGED to wrestle control of her thoughts away from the conversation with Mei Lu and turn them back to where they needed to be—on her case. Her father's suggestion came to the forefront of her thinking and ten minutes later she stood before the crime lab. She wasn't quite sure what she hoped to accomplish, yet something told her this was the place to start.

She walked inside with Grady's warning echoing in her mind.

Pulling out her badge, she flipped it in front of the receptionist's nose, then dropped it back into her purse. "I'm with SC," she said. "Need to check on some old cases. Gotta tech around I could talk to?"

The woman barely looked up from her computer screen. "Lawton Calvin's back there somewhere. Try his office, third door down the hall."

So much for security.

Risa muttered her thanks then headed quickly down the corridor, half-afraid the woman might call her back. She'd never heard of Calvin, but a few summers ago she'd worked closely with one of the techs on a serial rapist case and they'd developed a loose kind of camaraderie. Slinking down the hall with what she hoped was a low profile, Risa tried to remember the location of the woman's cubicle.

Before she could get too far, an officious-looking man with a bad comb-over stopped her. He wore a stained lab coat that had been white and gray tennis shoes that had been black. She didn't know him and, as far as she knew, he didn't recognize her, either. He certainly didn't seem happy to see her, though.

"I'm Lawton Calvin, the afternoon supervisor," he said. "Reception paged and said someone was coming back. May I help you?"

Risa gulped. "Actually I'm looking for a tech that helped me a while back. Her name was Sally—"

"Sally Bestow," he supplied. "Sally's no longer with us." His thin lips pressed together as if it hurt him to speak. "Did you have a question about a case?"

"Not exactly," she hedged.

He raised an eyebrow and waited.

She stumbled over her words. "I just wanted to review something with her...about your chain of custody and how evidence is handled, like from the M.E.'s office to here." She paused. "I'm aware of all the procedures, of course, and I know how everything works, but I had a theoretical question about evidence integrity."

"Then I'll give you a theoretical answer. It's secure." He smirked, clearly pleased with his answer. "Was there anything else?"

She ignored his attitude. "So blood evidence or something physical, like a weapon or say a slug... they're signed for each step of the way, aren't they? And...theoretically speaking, of course...one could trace who had handled each piece of evidence?"

He seemed to stiffen. "That's correct, more or less. Who did you say you are? I didn't catch your name—"

"I'm with S.C.," she answered. "I'm working on that case about the guy who beats up hookers."

She'd encountered men like Calvin before and there was only one way to handle them—by being a bully. He opened his mouth but she stopped him, drawing herself up to her full height and looking down at him. "Look here, Calvin, this is something I can't afford a leak on, okay? It's sensitive. If you mention this to anyone, there's going to be trouble. You need to forget I was even here."

"I'd be more than happy to forget this encounter."

"Thanks for nothing."

"My pleasure."

GRADY TOLD HIMSELF not to do it.

Even as he dialed her number, he was thinking, *I*

*shouldn't do this. This is stupid. What am I thinking
with?* Then she answered.

"It's me," Grady said. "I know it's late but—"

"It's okay," Risa replied. Her voice was softly
slurred and he knew he'd woken her. The thought
brought with it a slew of images and he enjoyed
every one of them.

"I went to see Melinda Rowling this afternoon."

"How's she doing?"

"Her housekeeping is suffering and her personal
hygiene could stand some improvement, but she
wasn't foaming at the mouth...until I mentioned
your name."

"Thanks for sharing. Is that what you called to tell
me?"

She hadn't invited him upstairs the night he'd been
to her house, but Grady could see Risa's bedroom in
his mind's eye. It'd be neat, orderly, no frills or ruf-
fles, just a bed. A big bed, wide enough for two.

"No," he finally answered, "that's not why I
called."

She waited but he didn't say more. "Am I supposed to guess the reason?"

"Can you?"

Her voice seemed to catch. "I probably could, but
should I?"

"I can't answer that. I've been doing a lot of

things lately that I shouldn't be doing, so maybe you need to ask someone else that question.''

"I'd rather ask you."

It's too late, he thought all at once. *I've gone too far and now it's too late. I can't go back.*

"I'm forty years old. You're twenty-six. That's fourteen years difference."

"You know your math."

"I'm investigating you for a serious crime. I have a responsibility to find out the truth."

"Absolutely."

"But I'm not sorry I kissed you this morning. I'm not going to apologize."

"I don't want you to."

"I wanted to make sure you understood that."

"I do." She waited and the silence grew again.

"There's more," he finally said.

"What is it?"

"I think Melinda Rowling's having an affair with another cop."

CHAPTER ELEVEN

RISA CAUGHT her breath and sat up in bed. She'd been thinking of Grady and their kiss. When she'd heard him on the other end, she'd almost freaked. Now this… "My God, are you sure?"

"No. I'm not sure, but I'd heard she was, and I went over there this afternoon. I wanted to decide for myself before I said anything."

"Did she admit to it?"

"Of course not. She lied like a big dog and threw me out of the house."

"How do you know she was lying?"

"IA men have built-in truth detectors. I could tell."

"Who's the guy?"

"*That* I don't know. Yet. I had been thinking it was Kinner, but she said it wasn't and she *was* telling the truth, then."

"Kinner or not, this is big, Grady. This could be the motivation you've been looking for. Maybe Melinda wanted to be with this other cop. They could have been working together to get rid of Luke and they set me up for it, just like Dad suggested. The officer's access would make the whole thing a snap.''

With sudden excitement, she swung her feet to the floor. ''Luke told me the night he got shot that she'd thrown him out and he couldn't go home. She'd called him names and told him not to come back.''

Pausing for a moment, Grady said, ''None of the other people I've interviewed have said anything about marital problems.''

''Luke wasn't a talker, at least not about his family.''

''Did he say why she kicked him out?''

''Not really. Just that they'd fought. And she wanted a divorce.''

''Why kill him if she'd already asked him for a divorce?'' He spoke as if to himself.

''Maybe there was a life-insurance policy. Maybe he would have fought her for the kid. Why does anyone kill their spouse instead of divorcing? If she and her lover did this, it certainly wouldn't be a first, would it?''

Another small silence built up, then he said, ''Why didn't you tell me about this earlier?''

Risa thought for a second. In her mind, Luke's fight with Melinda had been linked to his drinking, and Risa hadn't wanted to jeopardize his pension by mentioning either that night. But her own situation had changed since then. Because of the ballistics report and Melinda's accusations, there was now more at stake. She took a deep breath.

"Luke was drunk the night he died, Grady. In retrospect, maybe it wasn't a good idea but—"

"You're damn right, it wasn't a good idea. This is why you hesitated when I asked you if Luke used drugs, isn't it? You didn't want a screen done because you knew the family might lose his annuity if the truth got out. I admire your loyalty, but you should have known better, Risa." Suspicion tinged his voice. "Is there anything else you might have 'forgotten'?"

"No."

"Are you sure?"

He'd asked her the same thing this morning. Right before he'd told her not to investigate on her own. It was time to change the subject.

"Look, we need to concentrate on the problem at hand, not my memory. We need to find out who Melinda's been seeing. That's more important."

"*I* need to find out," he corrected her. "Me. Not you. Not even *we*. Do you hear me?" His voice rumbled with his warning, reminding Risa of the way he'd spoken to her at the church.

His cold voice brought her back to the moment. "I mean it, Risa. You're only going to make things harder on yourself. Leave the investigating to me."

GRADY CAUGHT Risa walking out of her office right before six the next evening. He'd deliberately waited until the end of the day to come see her, but the effort had been costly. Instead of working in the intervening hours, he'd stared at the clock. Last night, he'd come to the conclusion that he had to know—once and for all—if she and Luke had been lovers. Her revelation that Rowling had been drinking had been an eye-opener. What other secrets did she have? He told himself he had to know the truth because of what it meant to the case, but his need went beyond that. It was personal.

"Officer Taylor," he called out. "If you can spare a minute…"

She'd been saying good-night to the secretary he'd talked to that first day. Both women looked up as he came closer.

"I need to discuss a few things with you." He spoke formally then dipped his head to acknowledge the secretary. Her brown eyes gave him no quarter.

"Of course," Risa answered.

He took her by the elbow and maneuvered her out of earshot from the woman behind the desk. "I'd like to go somewhere quiet where we could talk. If you've got the time later tonight, do you think could we take a drive? Around nine or so?"

A momentary hesitation came across her features then it seemed to disappear. "That would be fine," she said in a noncommittal way. "I had something to do, but I can reschedule it."

He wondered reflexively if she had a date then he answered his own question, reminding himself if she'd been seeing anyone, he would know about it. He shook his head. What other kind of proof did he need to show how clouded his judgment had become?

He realized Risa was staring at him. "I'll see you at nine."

"I'll be waiting," she said.

HOW IN THE HELL could Grady have found out she'd managed to locate Sun and set up another meeting?

It seemed awfully coincidental that Grady had to see Risa tonight of all nights. But then again, who could say? More things than she liked to consider seemed to rest on luck and nothing else. She called the hooker on the way home and left a message on her machine. "I'll get back to you," she promised, "and we can schedule another time."

Fighting the traffic all the way from downtown to her neighborhood, she grabbed take-out Chinese from her usual place on the corner then drove home, munching on an egg roll. What did Grady want? Did he have something new to report on her case? Was he going to turn her loose?

Or arrest her?

The questions rattled around and grew, taking root in the fertile ground of her imagination. Maybe he'd learned the ballistics tests were wrong. Maybe Melinda had confessed to engineering the whole event. Maybe a terrible mistake had been made and nothing was what it seemed to be.

She finished eating when she got home, took a shower and changed. By the time she'd dried her hair and applied fresh makeup, it was almost nine. That's when she realized what she'd done. Without even thinking about it, she'd gotten ready as if for a date. She considered washing her face and combing her hair into a ponytail, but the doorbell rang. With a curse, she threw the lipstick she'd been about to put on into the sink and went downstairs.

Grady had replaced his coat and tie with a pair of jeans and a black short-sleeved shirt. He held a pair of sunglasses in one hand and a silk scarf in the other.

If this had been a date, they wouldn't have made it far. She would have dragged him right inside and then up the stairs. Along with his silk scarf.

She might just do it anyway.

"Are you up for a ride?" He tilted his head behind him and she came to her senses. His Porsche, with the top down, was parked in her driveway. He held up the scarf. "For your hair," he explained.

"I knew that," she said.

"Of course," he answered.

Five minutes later they were on the freeway and heading south. Grady was a skillful driver. As the traffic eased and the endless fast-food places and office complexes gave way to farmland, Risa found herself relaxing. If he'd come to tell her she was under arrest, he was certainly doing it the right way. She was almost sorry when he slowed the sports car and took the upcoming exit. Pulling into the parking lot of what looked like a down-home honky-tonk, he turned off the powerful engine and looked at her.

"Best country music for miles," he said, nodding his head toward the bar. "Coldest beers, too."

Risa simply stared at him. He was a cop who wore custom suits, taught college on the side and liked country music. Nothing about Grady fell into neat categories. As he opened her car door and helped her out, she decided she ought to stop trying to put him in a box. There wasn't one that would fit.

The place was almost empty. Lone Star beer signs flashed over a polished mahogany bar and at the other end of the room was a small stage. In between was a long wooden dance floor and a chicken-wire enclosure to protect the band, should there be one. A few rough men sat near the bar and an exhausted-looking salesman type took up one of the booths. The only other patrons, a couple, were seated near the back. They wore their guilt like bright red coats and

Risa wondered what their spouses were doing while they hid here and held hands.

Risa slid into the booth Grady indicated and issued a silent prayer of thanks that there was no band behind the cage. The idea of gliding across the dance floor doing the two-step with Grady was one she couldn't wrap her mind around. For one thing, she didn't want to get that close to him and for another...she didn't want to get that close to him.

Grady ordered a soft drink, but Risa needed something stronger. With some reservation, she took his suggestion and ordered a martini. Not wanting to hurt the waitress's feelings, she waited until the woman had left to say, "Are you sure?"

He nodded confidently. "It'll be fine, I promise."

They made small talk until the bleached blonde returned with their drinks. Risa took one sip, then arched her eyebrows as the martini slid down her throat in a fine cold rush.

"I told you," he said. "One of these days you'll start to believe what I say."

She took another sip then set her glass down. "I'm afraid that day might be closer than you think."

"Why is that?"

Instead of answering, she reached into her purse and pulled out a dollar bill, pushing it toward him. "I owe you this."

He made no move to take the money.

"Your friends disappeared on you," he said softly.

She nodded, her throat stinging. And she couldn't blame the drink. "I talked to the last one today. I thought she could help me with—"

She stopped but it was too late. He already understood what she'd done; she could read it in his eyes. She finished her sentence quietly. "I thought she might tell me something about David Kinner, but she didn't know him."

"No one seems to be on your side anymore."

She nodded. Giving her a moment, he took a drink and stayed silent. She appreciated the fact that he didn't try to analyze the situation or give her advice. When he changed the subject, she appreciated it even more.

"I submitted your protest to my boss."

"So you didn't bring me out here to arrest me?"

"I wouldn't take you for a ride then throw the cuffs on you. That'd be too cruel, even for me."

"Actually, I thought it might be a nice way to break the news." She took another swallow of her martini. "How much more time is this going to take, though?"

"My captain will sit on your protest for a while. Then we'll have a meeting. Then another one." He shrugged. "I can't answer that question. I have no idea. Because of who you are, they'll drag their feet before filing any charges."

She caught her breath, then let it out slowly. "Did you ever find out anything about Kinner? I know you said he's not Melinda's lover but I still think he threw the brick."

"I think he had something to do with it, too. I did some checking and the timing fits. Plus, I got the lab to confirm that your brick came from the same batch as the ones on his lake house."

"Grady! Why didn't you tell me this earlier?"

"Because it doesn't matter. Kinner's too dumb to plan a dognapping much less a complicated frame-up job. In addition, he has no motive. Unless you're crazy, being pissed about a promotion isn't a good enough motivation to kill someone. And Kinner isn't crazy. He's just stupid. He deposited five hundred dollars cash into his checking account the day after your window was shattered. I'm working the possibilities, but I need to find out where that money came from before I do anything else."

His expression shifting, Grady reached across the table and covered her hand with his. "Forget about Kinner. He doesn't matter. I brought you out here for another reason, and it's important I have the truth. I've asked you this question before, but it's do or die time now."

She sat as still as she could, her heart racing inside her chest. "What do you want to know?"

"Were you and Luke having an affair?"

Her relief was so palpable, she knew Grady could see it.

"No." Her eyes locked on his. "I never slept with Luke. I don't mess around with married men…" She had started to add her usual *or cops,* but what was the point? "We were *not* lovers."

From somewhere in the back, a jukebox switched to a slow song. Grady seemed to sit in judgment for a moment, then relief, or something damn close to it, came and went across his face.

"Let's dance," he said.

With a what-the-hell shrug, Risa slid from the booth and joined him on the empty wooden floor.

When the song finished, they continued to sway and in a second, another one started up. Five tracks later, Risa had lost what little will she'd had to stay out of Grady's arms. Instead, she felt as if she never wanted to leave them.

He looked down at her. She could have been wrong, but his expression seemed to reflect her own desire.

"Let's get out of here," he said. "I want to be alone with you."

"I'm not sure that's such a good idea."

"I didn't say it was. But I still want to do it."

Leaving enough cash on the table for their drinks and a tip, he grabbed her hand and they walked out to the Porsche.

As soon as they were in front seat, Grady pulled Risa to him and began to kiss her.

Her mouth was as soft as he remembered, her skin as fragrant. She wasn't the kind of woman who went for heavy perfume and he was glad—her natural scent was heady enough. Lifting her over the gearbox, he brought her into his lap and she curled around him like a cat, her hands behind his head, her tongue coming out to tease his own. The feel of her body against his made him moan, and suddenly he felt like an eighteen-year-old kid in the back seat with a girl for the very first time.

Except for one big difference.

He'd been in a roaring hurry at that age, but Grady knew better now. He took his time and slowly savored each sensation. The lingering taste of gin on her lips, the tiny groans she made as she snuggled closer, the satin feel of her hair. He took off her jacket then eased one of the thin straps of her camisole down, pressing his lips against the hollow of her collarbone. Grady had never tasted an angel, but he knew right then and there, one couldn't be any better than this.

He kissed his way back to her mouth as his hands dropped to her breasts. Beneath the fabric of her top, her nipples stood up and he gently rubbed a thumb over first one and then the other. Her breasts were full and pear-shaped and he was just about to dip his hand inside her camisole when the distant ringing of a cell phone penetrated the fog of his desire.

Cursing loudly, Grady fumbled for the phone at his waistband. Risa started to move away, but he grabbed her and held her still, somehow shaking the phone open with his other hand and answering. "Wilson here."

He sounded out of breath—hell, he *was* out of breath—but Samuel Andrews didn't seem to notice. The homicide lieutenant had more important things on his mind.

"We got trouble," Andrews said without preamble. "The hospital just called and something's happened with John Doe Two. We gotta get there fast."

"Shit." Releasing Risa, Grady ran a hand through his hair. "Is he conscious? Has he said anything—"

"I don't have time to explain. Meet me at Ben Taub as soon as you can."

"I'm on my way."

Grady snapped the phone shut, then looked across the seat at Risa.

"I've got to get to the medical center. Something's going down with John Doe Two."

RISA CLIMBED back to her side of the car, where she grabbed her jacket then slipped her arms into the sleeves. "I'm coming with you."

His hand on the key, Grady looked at her. "No, you're not."

"But I have—"

"I'll call you after I get more details," he said firmly. The engine roared to life and he put the car in gear.

"But—"

He shook his head. "No buts, Risa. You can't come with me and you know it, so why are you even asking?"

She wanted to scream *because it means so much,* but they hit the freeway at eighty, and above the roar of the wind, any conversation became impossible.

Forced into silence, Risa fumed. She understood Grady's position, but she needed to know what was happening, dammit! Her whole future depended on it.

They arrived back at her house quicker than she would have thought possible. She argued her case the entire time Grady walked her to the front door. When they got to her steps, he lifted her chin, stared down at her and said two words. "I'm sorry."

"You're 'sorry'?" she repeated angrily. "'Sorry' isn't good enough, Grady. You need to take me with you."

"I can't do that, Risa, and you know it."

"But—"

He lowered his head and cradled her face between

his hands, kissing her with such passion that he almost made her forget the argument. Almost.

She looked up at him breathlessly. "Grady... please."

His eyes went cold then he kissed her again, hard and fast. "I'll call you."

Standing on her front porch until the taillights of the Porsche had faded, Risa went inside, frustrated and angry. Her knees were trembling, she realized unexpectedly, and an emotion that was at once empty and foreign stormed inside her. She wasn't sure if she was more angry because Grady had had to leave or because he wouldn't take her with him.

Either way, every nerve was on full stand-up alert. She slammed into the kitchen, grabbed the first glass in the cabinet, a cheap plastic one, and poured herself a drink of water. She guzzled it as if it were the martini she'd left behind, then she set the glass down so hard, the plastic cracked.

She picked it up and glared at it. The surface had remained intact but the plastic itself was completely cracked, a thousand spiderwebs of weakness now threatening its integrity. Lifting her eyes, she stared blindly out the window over the sink, a set of headlights sweeping through the darkness as a car took off. She looked back down at her hands. The damn glass was a perfect metaphor for her entire life.

She was holding herself together, but just barely. With the slightest nudge, she would shatter.

Opening her fingers, Risa let the tumbler fall into the sink. It bounced once, rolled toward the center, then came to a stop on its side.

She turned with a sigh and went upstairs, but she didn't even try to sleep. Instead, she called Grady too many times to count. Each time, he had no news. She gave up at three then two hours later, her phone rang.

Grady sounded strange, his voice strained. "He's dead."

"Shit!" Disappointment rippled over her as she sat up in the bed. "Did he say anything before he went? Please tell me he said something."

"He didn't tell us a damn thing." He paused. "He was gone before we got there."

"What about an ID?"

"His name is Ricardo Sanchez. Andrews said he has a sheet three miles long. I've ordered a copy of it—"

"Stop right there," she interrupted, her voice incredulous. "If the guy had a sheet, why has it taken us this long to ID him? We should have had his name the day Luke got shot. Please don't tell me he wasn't printed."

"He *was* printed, but somewhere between the hospital and headquarters, the cards got lost. Nobody realized what had happened until he died and the morgue printed him again.''

Grady paused, an undercurrent in his silence something she couldn't ignore. Gripping the phone with both hands, she carefully swung her feet to the floor. ''So what *aren't* you saying, Grady?''

''Somebody came into his hospital room and smothered him with a pillow. He didn't just die—he was murdered.''

Risa's mouth fell open. ''Oh, my God. What… When…''

''The staff was holding a meeting when one of the nurses realized she'd left something in his room. She went back to get it and caught a guy in a mask beside the bed. He knocked her out with a sap then finished the job he'd started. They locked down the hospital as soon as they discovered her, but he was long gone by the time she came to and explained what had happened.''

''We didn't have a guard on Sanchez,'' she said.

''There was no reason to.''

''I'm coming down there.''

''No!'' He lowered his voice and spoke again. ''Don't even think about it, Risa.''

''But, Grady—''

''Don't do it.'' She'd never heard the tone his voice now held. ''If you show up, I swear to God, Risa, I'll arrest you myself. Do you understand me?''

She exhaled slowly. "I understand."

"Don't say a word about this to anyone, either." He repeated himself and said, *"Anyone,"* then he hung up.

There would be no more sleeping.

In a daze, Risa got up and dressed. All she felt was confusion, a thousand questions running through her head. Clearly someone had a stake in keeping Sanchez quiet, but who? And why? Could Kinner have done this? She felt a tiny bit of hope, but it was quickly followed by a dose of reality. Until she got more information, she simply couldn't understand the situation completely. After a fast cup of microwaved coffee, she went into the office. She'd been there a little more than an hour when a man appeared in her doorway. Looking up in surprise, she met her father's eyes.

"I've got some info for you," he said without any other greeting. "But you didn't hear it from me."

She'd called him right after talking to Mei Lu. It had been another one of those awkward conversations and when she'd hung up, Risa had wondered why she'd phoned him in the first place. He'd said so little she'd wondered if she'd imagined the closeness she'd felt the day she'd stopped at the house.

"Okay." She motioned him to a chair across from her desk. She thought of telling him about the shooter, but then Grady's warning came right behind it. She stayed quiet.

"You told me the other day that you'd learned someone wasn't being faithful. You remember who that was?"

He clearly didn't want to speak Melinda Rowling's name out loud. Risa felt her skin prickle at his cautiousness. "Yes, I do."

"I know the identity of someone who might be connected to that situation."

This time it took her a second, but she finally got it. "You know who her...accomplice is?"

"I do and you do, too."

She'd been rocking back in her chair, but all at once, Risa froze.

"You made his acquaintance at an inauspicious time the other day. I wasn't there but I heard about it later. He was sitting right by her and holding her hand."

Risa thought for a minute, then sucked in her breath. Kurt Trundle had been next to Melinda on the couch when she'd attacked Risa. A few days later, he'd made a point of speaking to her at the range. If he were Melinda Rowling's lover, it could explain a lot. And raise some more questions, as well.

"Are you sure about this?" she asked her father.

"I'm sure of the information. What it means is something you're going to have to handle."

He stood up before she could thank him, then walked out the door.

GRADY STEPPED from the shower to the sound of his doorbell ringing. Something about the way it buzzed told him the finger that was on it had been there for a while. He wrapped a towel around his waist and slung another over his shoulder. "I'm coming, I'm coming."

Risa stood on the doorstep.

She took in his lack of clothing and wet hair. It looked for a second as if she had something caught in her throat then she composed herself.

"I'm sorry," she said. "I should have called, but this is important. May I come in?"

Without waiting for his answer, she brushed past him and walked into his entry.

"Sure," he said, closing the door behind her. "Please…come on in and make yourself at home."

She turned and met his eyes. There was no humor in her gaze, just steely determination.

"I want to know more about the shooter's murder, but I have to tell you something first. I know who Melinda Rowling's lover is," she said abruptly. "He's a guy by the name of Kurt Trundle. He's on the—"

"—the SWAT team." He finished her sentence, his mind in a sudden turmoil. "How do you know this?"

"My father told me. After I got to my office this morning, he dropped by."

Grady hid his surprise. "How does *he* know?"

"I didn't bother to ask," she replied, "because he wouldn't have told me. He may not be on the payroll anymore, but he always protects his sources."

A flashbulb went off in Grady's mind and for some reason, he remembered The Call. "Does your father have a dog?" he asked without warning.

Risa frowned. "No, but sometimes he keeps my brother's fiancée's mutt. Why on earth—"

Grady waved off her question "It's not important," he said. "Just tell me this—do you believe him?"

"We don't get along, but my dad isn't a person who screws around. He said it was the truth so, yes, I do believe him."

"He wants to help you."

Risa's jaw went tight. "He wants to protect the family's reputation."

Grady sat down on his sofa, wet towel and all. Risa sat beside him, her voice turning urgent. "You said Kinner was too dumb to plan something like this, but Kurt Trundle doesn't look like he would fall into that category. If he and Melinda were lovers and they wanted Luke out of the way, he could figure out a way to set me up. Trundle's been on the edge of this thing from the very beginning. He could have even been the one who gave Kinner the money you saw deposited in his account.''

Grady met her eyes and shook his head. ''He's not on the edge, Risa. He's right smack-dab in the middle of it.''

CHAPTER TWELVE

GRADY TOOK her hands, his expression more serious than she'd ever seen it. Her fingers looked small in his larger grip and suddenly Risa didn't feel as confident as she had when she'd burst through his door.

"I didn't tell you this before now for reasons I can't explain, but I have a tape," he said. "From the security cameras at Tequila Jack's."

Risa felt her mouth fill with dust as she imagined reliving that moment, even if just by video. "Are you saying the shooting was filmed?"

Dropping her fingers, he stood to walk across the room to a series of bookcases and cabinets that spanned the length of the wall. "The camera was programmed to take snapshots of the area at timed intervals. It didn't catch the actual shooting, but it caught a lot."

Her pulse wasn't just pounding, it was roaring inside her ears. His words seemed to come from a distance.

"Why didn't you tell me this earlier?" she asked faintly.

"I have my reasons." The way he spoke told her he wasn't going to explain.

"Then why tell me now?"

"I probably shouldn't have but you surprised me with Trundle's name. He's on the tape. He was there that night."

She frowned in confusion, then she cleared her expression. "SWAT came—after the shooting…"

He nodded. "Dispatch hears a 10-33 and a 10-18 together, they're gonna get everyone on deck. Rowling sounded panicky and they wanted to cover their bases."

Risa understood. When an officer requested help—urgent help—it was considered serious. Luke couldn't have known at that point that the men had guns, but he'd been asleep, she reminded herself. And drunk. His judgment would have been completely off, his mind in chaos.

"Do you know Trundle?" she asked.

"I've met him," Grady said. "How about you?"

"I didn't before the incident at Melinda's, but a few days after that, I saw him at the range. I thought then it was just a coincidental meeting, but maybe it wasn't."

"You think he was following you?"

"I don't know. He could have just seen me and decided he'd yank my chain a bit. He gave me his card."

"Why?"

Risa explained, but Grady was shaking his head before she'd even finished.

"You think it was a come-on?" she asked. "That doesn't make sense if he and Melinda are an item."

"I don't think *any* of this makes sense," Grady answered. "But I know for sure that he was there the night Luke was killed. And you think he was sleeping with Luke's wife. Those two things are enough to make me wonder."

She crossed the room and put her fingertips on his bare chest. "Would you show me the tape?"

His expression started to close. "That wouldn't be a good idea, Risa."

"I told you that last night, but you didn't listen to me. You took me to your car and kissed me anyway." She flattened her palms against his skin. "Why should I listen to you?"

"Because this is different." He covered her fingers with his, twining them together and gripping them tightly. "I don't want you to get hurt any more than you already have been."

His answer should have surprised her, but it didn't. She'd already begun to see, if not acknowledge, the man behind the IA rules.

"I can handle it," she said.

"I'm sure you can. But it isn't necessary. Kurt was

there. You can take my word for it or ask Andrews. He'll confirm it.''

''I believe you,'' she said, ''but I still want to view the tape.''

His eyes went over her shoulders as if he were considering her request—or lying. When they came back to her face, their color had chilled. ''I don't have the tape here. It's at the office.''

She wanted to argue but knew it would be useless. He wasn't going to give in.

''All right.'' She dragged out the syllables. ''I'll accept that for now. Where do we go from here?''

''*WE* DON'T go anywhere.'' Tightening his towel, Grady stepped around Risa. ''You're leaving and then I'll decide the next step. It'll probably involve putting a tail on Melinda Rowling and Trundle.'' He padded into the entry and waited at the front door for Risa to follow. ''You're leaving,'' he repeated in a louder voice.

When she didn't appear, he reversed his direction. She was in the same spot.

''I'm not going anywhere.'' She crossed her arms. ''If you want to get rid of me, you'll have to throw me out.''

''Risa, c'mon! I've got to get dressed then I have to decide how I'm going to handle this. I want you out of here.'' When she didn't move, he put his hand on his towel as if he were about to pull it off. "I'm warning you…"

She dropped her gaze to the knot where his fingers rested, then she lifted her eyes to his. "I grew up with three brothers. You haven't got anything under there I haven't seen before."

Cursing loudly, Grady turned around, ripped off the towel and headed for his bedroom.

Standing in front of his closet, he yanked on a pair of jeans. She was right behind him when he turned to get a shirt.

"I can't just stand on the sidelines, Grady. This is tearing me up inside."

He put his hands on her shoulders with a sigh. "Risa," he said measuredly, "do you understand just how many rules and regulations I've already broken? You're a smart woman so you must know. Are you trying to get us fired?" He didn't give her time to answer. "You must be. That's the only reason I can think of that you'd insist on being included in your own damn investigation."

For a second—one fleeting second—he thought she might start crying, but she didn't. Instead, she looked him straight in the eye.

They were inches apart, so close he could feel her breath when she spoke. "If that's the only reason you can think of, then let me give you a few more."

She moved a millimeter closer. He didn't know if

he should take advantage of her nearness and try to kiss her or be worried for his safety.

"My job is my life." She spoke slowly and deliberately, her manner as set as her expression. "I don't have a husband. I don't have kids. Hell, I don't even have a dog. All my so-called friends have abandoned me and I'm on my own. If I'm not completely exonerated by this investigation, I might as well quit. My career is the only thing I care about, and I'm not going to abandon what little control over it I have left. Not to you. Not to anyone. I can't."

She stopped to take a breath, and that's when something appeared in her expression that he hadn't seen before now.

It was desperation.

And his heart cracked open.

He slipped his hand behind her hair, his fingers curling around her neck. "You should give me a chance, Risa. I can help you. I'm good at what I do."

"So was I," she said tightly. "But no one remembers that now."

GRADY CLOSED his eyes as if it hurt him to hear her words. When he opened them, she read his surrender and a flush of hope came over her.

"Let me finish dressing," he said. "I'm not promising you anything, but we'll talk." He tilted his head. "Go wait for me in the living room. I can't think straight with you standing so close to my bed."

His obvious desire warmed her, but his acceptance of her plea meant even more. Risa put her hand on his stubbled jaw then she kissed him. "Thank you," she whispered.

He kissed her back, then said, "Go fix us some coffee or read the paper or whatever. I'll be done in a minute."

"I'll be waiting." Returning to the living room, Risa wandered around the room, her mind a thousand miles away. When she finally stopped pacing, she found herself in front of the huge cabinet where Grady had stood a few minutes before. She assumed it hid his television and stereo equipment and she shook her head. What was it about men and their televisions? The double doors in the center were ajar and, without thinking, she reached out to close them. But they wouldn't shut.

She pulled them open and the reason was immediately obvious. An empty cardboard tape case protruded from between the television set and the side of the cabinet. She reached in to push it back and the familiar label caught her eye.

The case was from the HPD crime lab. The date and case number, as always, had been printed on the side. *Security Camera No. 1* was written just below, then the time—*3:00 a.m–5:00 a.m.*

Her eyes flew to the VCR where the tape was in the slot. She caught her breath as her heart began to hammer. Grady had lied. He'd told her he didn't have the surveillance tape, but here it was.

Her hand trembled as she pushed in the cartridge and turned on the television set.

The black-and-white scene was grainy, the images jerky. They stuttered past in a broken sequence. She recognized the parking lot of the club and the entrance, people coming and going. The picture then skipped a bit and blurred. The crime lab had clearly worked on the tape to eliminate dead space. When the recording slowed and focused again, she saw herself coming around the corner of the building.

A knot of pain began to build inside her chest. The tape sped up again and more patrons walked into the bar, then the door burst open to reveal Risa pushing the two suspects ahead of her.

She tensed, waiting for what happened next.

Just as Grady had said, the few seconds of the shooting itself had not been captured, but the aftermath had. Her fingers over her mouth, Risa watched as she kneeled beside Luke on the now-bloody sidewalk and tried to get a pulse. No sound had been recorded, of course, but none was necessary.

Sinking to the floor in front of the television set, Risa stared at the screen in disbelief. Flooded with adrenaline at the time, then with grief and confusion later, she had only relived the tragedy in her dreams. Seeing it now, the details so stark and the results so permanent, she felt the facade of strength she'd been able to maintain slowly disintegrate. Unlike the glass in her kitchen last night, she shattered into a thousand separate pieces, each one sharp as a razor.

"SHIT." Grady's curse was whispered but he could have screamed it and Risa would never have noticed.

He walked quickly to the VCR and shut it off. Wide-eyed with shock, pale with disbelief, Risa continued to stare at the screen, even though it had turned solid blue.

"You didn't need to see that," he said.

She didn't reply.

He took her elbow and pulled her to her feet, the movement jarring her out of her silent agony.

"I was wrong," she said without inflection.

"About what?"

She looked up at him. "I said I could handle it, but I was wrong. I shouldn't have watched that."

Leading her to the couch, he sat and pulled her down beside him, putting his arm around her, his sympathy for her welling up from a source he couldn't control. He knew he was about to make a terrible mistake, but he really didn't care.

"You never give yourself a break, Risa," he said. "Why didn't you just let it slide for once?"

Her eyes were huge and filled with pain. "I learned to be tough when I was a kid and the lesson has stayed with me. I'm afraid to let up now. Who knows what would happen?"

"You might be surprised."

"I doubt that." She turned her head slightly and looked at the television set. "I might not have a choice anymore, though. This one…this one's gonna be hard to beat."

Her voice caught on the last word, and the desire to comfort her overtook his common sense. He pulled her to him and kissed her, his mouth fitting perfectly over hers. She put her arms around his neck, a low murmur escaping from the back of her throat.

She needed him, he thought in a daze. The independent, strong-willed woman who intimidated men who intimidated *other* men, needed him. She needed his strength, his encouragement, his ability to make things okay.

She needed him.

And Grady knew that wasn't right.

CLINGING TO GRADY, Risa deepened the kiss he'd started, her tongue slipping into his mouth, the last of her misgivings disappearing as her passion grew. She wanted him to make her forget what she'd just seen. If he didn't, she'd have the images in her head forever. Despite her earlier speech, suddenly the cost didn't matter to her. She was ready to pay any price to stop the pain.

Their kiss eased into something other than consolation, though. His mouth turned even more insistent than it had been last night in the parking lot, and Risa felt herself falling into a place she wasn't sure she could find her way out of. Then she wondered why she'd ever want to.

He lowered her to the couch, his mouth never leaving hers as his hand went beneath her blouse and caressed her bare skin, his fingers sliding upward to her bra. Etching a path around the lace cup, he started to groan just as she found the buttons on his shirt. Undoing them one by one, Risa stopped long enough to allow him to lift her blouse and pull it over her head, then she peeled off his shirt. She spread her hands over his bare chest and the smattering of dark hair that covered it. Putting her face against him, she willed time to stop. If she never moved again, she'd die a happy woman.

Grady didn't allow that to happen.

He brought his hands to her shoulders and tipped her face up, his expression and his body shifting subtly. She wouldn't have noticed if she hadn't been holding him so tightly, but beneath her fingers, his muscles grew taut and corded, and even his jaw turned to stone. His eyes, so strange to begin with, seemed to become a different color.

Desire, dark and swift, sparked deep within her and everything began to shift, including her need for solace. The segue wasn't smooth, either. A violent shudder ripped through her as she looked into his gaze. Tottering on the edge of a cliff she'd never been to before, she realized that Grady had initiated the change deliberately. He read the dawning comprehension in her expression and that was all the confirmation he needed. The air between them heated and then ignited. Neither of them cared what was burned in the process.

Kissing her forcefully, Grady removed her bra so quickly Risa heard something tear. He then put both his hands around her breasts and his mouth found her nipples. With her fingers digging into his back, he kissed then bit her right breast, his teeth softly scraping at her skin. The feeling was an exquisite combination of pain and desire. Everything but the need for fulfillment fled Risa's mind.

Her fingers reached for the silver buckle on his belt and she began to unfasten it, the cool metal warming beneath her feverish hands. A second later, his pants were off, then so were hers.

Rolling to one side, Grady caught his slacks before they hit the floor. Thrusting his hand into the right pocket, he pulled a small Mylar packet from his wallet then placed it on the cushion beside them. The whole time, he kept his arm around Risa's bare shoulders, his eyes never leaving hers.

He didn't put the condom on. Instead, he slid down her body, his mouth tracing the path his fingers had taken earlier. She didn't want the torture to stop, but she couldn't wait for him to move on, either. His hands drew paths of fire over her skin. By the time he raised himself above her, Risa's breathing had ceased and her heart felt as if it might explode. He tore open the package with his teeth then handed her the condom. She rolled it over him and a moment later he was inside her.

The sensation was exquisite, but it was the look in his eyes she knew she'd always remember. Later she'd search for a word to describe it, but at that very moment all she could do was let the experience wash over her. Cold and hot. Frightening and comforting. Familiar and strange. The sensations flashed between them in a heartbeat, then Grady's rhythm quickened. When Risa climaxed, she screamed his name.

HE LEFT THE ROOM so she could dress in private. After the intimacies they'd just shared, Grady wasn't quite sure why he felt the need to do this, but he didn't examine his motivation closely. There were too many other issues racing around inside what was left of his brain to give the thought the consideration it was due. Issues like how her career would be over if anyone found out what had just happened. Issues like whether or not he should even continue on the case. Issues like how stupid they'd both been.

He had to admit the truth, though. He hadn't stopped when he'd realized comfort wasn't what Risa had needed. The emotions she was dealing with were too traumatic, too life-changing to be handled so delicately. She'd had to have sweeping passion, passion so overwhelming that it momentarily took her to another place and time. He'd tried to give her just that, but like an out-of-control blaze, the flames had consumed him, too. Their entire relationship had been dangerous in ways he didn't want to think about, but now they'd risked everything to sate their passion.

Facing the other direction, Risa was buttoning her blouse when he returned. Putting his hands on her shoulders, he brought her back against his chest and buried his face in the silk of her hair, wrapping his arms around her from behind.

"What have we done, Risa?" he murmured. "What in the hell have we done?"

She turned in his embrace and lifted her eyes to his. Her expression was different, he thought, softer somehow and more open, but as she spoke, a flash of apprehension came over her features before she could hide it. "Please don't tell me you regret this."

"Oh, God." He pulled her against him and spoke above her head. "Why in the hell would I say something like that?"

"I don't know." Her voice was muffled as she spoke. "Maybe because you might feel that way?"

"Never." He shook his head. "If I live to be a thousand years old, I'll never regret this." Bringing his hands to her cheeks, he cradled her face with tenderness, emotions flooding him that he couldn't ignore no matter how much he wanted to. "You're a helluva woman, Risa. There's so much more to you than I realized." He paused and searched for the right words.

She closed her eyes. "Don't say that word, either. I hate that word."

"What word?"

"The one that's coming next. *But…*"

As she spoke, his throat closed. She opened her eyes and there was resignation in them. She stepped away from him and cursed softly. "Dammit, Grady…"

He tried to draw her back but she resisted his tug. "I shouldn't have let this happen," he said. "I should have stopped us, but I didn't. We can*not* do this again."

She turned. "What difference does it make now? We're in so deep…"

"*I* am," he said, "but I don't really give a crap about my career anymore. You do. And you should. You still have a chance at keeping it as long as no one finds out."

"Grady—"

"I'm not just talking about this, Risa." He tilted his head to the couch behind them. "The sex is the least of what I've done wrong."

Their eyes met.

"It's a little late to point this out now, but I've told you things I shouldn't have. I've let you know details of the case. I've done everything wrong that could possibly be done wrong. I don't want to prove your innocence only to have some idiot question the outcome because of how we've acted. Someone could and you know it."

He stalked away from her. His heart felt as heavy as the burden he'd been carrying, the burden of proving her innocence. He'd never wanted to clear an officer as much as he wanted to clear Risa, but that very desire could be her undoing, not to mention his own.

His back stiff, he stared out his front window then he spoke without turning.

"Go home, Risa. Go home and let me do my job."

SHE ALMOST MADE IT to her house without breaking down.

Somewhere between the end of her street and her driveway, though, a stupid song popped into Risa's head. Her brothers had been into country music during the '80s and the radio had stayed on a station that only played songs featuring steel guitars and heartbroken cowboys. The tunes had driven her crazy.

The actual words to the song escaped her, but the sentiment was clear. The disconsolate woman who'd sung it was crying because loving her man was wrong…but it felt so right.

Parking her car, Risa put her head against the steering wheel, the words repeating themselves inside her brain over and over and over. She'd thought her life was spinning out of control before this, but tonight she'd actually seen it disappear down the drain. Grady was right. If anyone found out they'd slept together, her career in law enforcement would be over, not to mention his. Despite its size, the community was a close one. Everyone would know.

If loving you is wrong… If loving you is wrong…

A bubble of hysteria rose inside her and came to the surface. She started to laugh, then something else happened and her eyes began to sting. Her throat went tight and all at once, her chest hurt.

She reminded herself that Taylors never cried.

Lifting her head, she stared out a windshield that was suddenly blurry. She clearly wasn't a Taylor anymore.

STAN RICHARDS THREW a hissy fit at Grady's request for a tail on Melinda Rowling and Kurt Trundle, but in the end, he relented...sort of. Approving the expense for two days, his boss made it clear Grady would get nothing more. Grady understood. He only got what he did because Richards didn't want to look bad in front of the chief should Trundle's involvement be proved. Two days of surveillance were worthless unless they got lucky but either way, Richards could claim success. After checking Trundle's work schedule, Grady put one man on Melinda and one on the SWAT cop on his first day off.

Nothing happened.

On the third day Trundle put in for a vacation day for the following Friday. Grady hadn't spoken to Risa since they'd made love because he didn't know what to say to her. He still didn't, but that afternoon, he called her.

He didn't bother to say hello. "I've had a tail on Melinda and Trundle for two days, but we've gotten zip," he said when Risa answered her phone. "I'm going to follow them myself on Friday. I'll let you know what happens."

If she was nonplussed by his lack of phone manners, Risa didn't show it. "Let me come," she said instead.

"Absolutely not," he answered firmly. "Things have been screwed up enough already, Risa. I'm not going to compound the issue."

"Please, Grady. I...I'm going crazy. I've got to do...something."

"I let us do something already." His reference to their lovemaking was clear. "We can't afford a repeat, Risa."

"I understand," she said quietly. "That's not what I want, either."

An arc of pain stabbed him as she spoke. He softened his voice. "I didn't say I didn't want it, Risa. I said we can't afford it. Don't twist my words. You know what I mean—I'm talking about us being seen together. Not what happened between us."

"I knew exactly what you meant, Grady. *You're* the one who turned the words around. The truth is I don't care about what happened between us. It was over before it even started."

He'd been in IA way too long not to recognize a lie when he heard one. But Grady had never fallen in love with a cop he was investigating, either. Maybe he thought she was lying because that's what he wanted to think.

"All I'm concerned about is my career," she continued. "If I don't take the risk and try to help myself, I won't have anything at all later. I told you this the other day and nothing's changed. You've *got* to let me help. It's the only thing I have left.''

Truth or not, he didn't know which hurt him more—her denial of what they'd shared or the searing pain in her voice. He put the choice out of his mind. ''And if someone spots us?''

''You can lie and say you were interviewing me again.'' She paused, her jaw tightening. ''I've got to see for myself, Grady. I've got to be sure.''

''Pick me up at ten,'' he said gruffly. ''We'll take your car. Melinda won't recognize it.''

BEFORE THEY GOT to the end of the block Friday morning, Grady pointed to a convenience store with a phone booth out front. ''Stop there,'' he said. ''I want to make sure she's at home before we start this wild-goose chase.''

Risa followed his instructions then watched as he crossed the parking lot to the kiosk and inserted a handful of coins. He wore a pair of pressed jeans and a dark blue T-shirt. The jeans hugged his narrow hips and the shirt made his eyes seem darker. Despite what she'd told him over the phone, Risa had thought constantly about what had happened between them. She knew in her heart nothing between them was over, and she suspected, no matter how the investigation ended, the situation would stay that way forever. Grady had tunneled into the deepest part of who Risa really was and he was there to stay.

What made him so damn attractive? Was it his power? Was it his age? Was it his body? All three? The thought of spending hours alone with him doing surveillance had almost sent her over the edge, but her career was in the balance, so nothing short of a nuclear reaction would have kept her away. Still, it was going to be a long day.

He opened the car door and slid inside. "She's there. Let's go."

On the way over, Grady outlined the route he wanted their surveillance to take. He didn't stop talking until Risa exited the Southwest Freeway and wound her way to Luke's subdivision.

"Any questions?" he asked.

Her mind had returned to their lovemaking, and she hadn't heard a word.

"No questions," she answered.

He didn't reply. Stopping the car five houses down from the Rowlings, Risa parked the Toyota, relief sweeping over her that he hadn't pressed the issue.

She should have known better.

He was quiet for a moment more then she felt his stare move from the house to her profile. He spoke slowly. "Actually, I'm not too sure about that last part of the plan. Do you think that's the best way to handle it? What would you do if you were Melinda and we did that?"

She turned to face him.

"I don't have a chance in hell of getting the answer to that question right and you know it. I wasn't listening to a word you said."

"Why not?"

"Why do you think?"

He looked away from her and said nothing. After a while, he reached over the seat and drew a line down the back of her hand. His soft touch left a fevered trail that did nothing to clear up her mounting frustration.

He spoke softly. "Why don't you talk for both of us. Otherwise, we're going to drive ourselves crazy."

She didn't know if she felt better or worse to know he shared her confusion. She bit her bottom lip then released it and began to speak.

CHAPTER THIRTEEN

"I ALWAYS WANTED to be a cop," she said. "I grew up hearing my brothers and father talk about the life and I never considered doing anything else."

He sighed inwardly with relief. If she wanted to talk about her childhood, it was fine by him. Just about anything she wanted to do was turning out to be fine by him. Unfortunately.

"I've heard rumors about you and your dad. That he didn't really want you to join the force. Is that right?"

"I thought you knew everything about me," she said. "Wasn't that in my file?"

He shook his head. "Afraid not."

"Well, it should be because it's the truth. The son of a bitch didn't even go to my graduation."

Her words were tinged with more sadness than anger and he wondered if she knew.

"He went to my brothers'. But not to mine."

"Have you ever asked him why?"

"I don't need to—he made his feelings clear."
She flicked her gaze in his direction then back toward

the Rowlings' house. Her glance was fast but not fast enough for him to miss the pain in her eyes. "He never thought I was good enough for the force. And he still doesn't."

"Because you're a woman?"

"Probably. Who knows?" She shrugged. "Who cares?"

"You do," he said quietly.

Her expression closed and her profile went stony. "You couldn't be any further from the truth. I learned a long time ago that my brothers were my dad's priority. I came in a distant fourth, after them, his job and his '58 Chevy." She shook her head, her dark hair glinting in the summer sun. "He doesn't know it, but I made a deal with him after my graduation. I don't want his approval anymore and, in return, he never gives it."

Before Grady could pursue the issue, she turned the tables on him. "So what was your ex's problem? You told me she didn't want you to be a cop, either. Couldn't she handle the hours?"

Risa's interpretation of his failed marriage made Grady laugh. "My hours were the least of her concern. In fact, she worked more than I did. It got to where we never even saw each other, but that was okay with me because whenever we did get any time together, she'd use it to launch into her you-don't-make-enough-money routine, which was always followed by her your-job-stinks-and-isn't-prestigious-enough routine.''

"She was right.''

"I know, but that doesn't mean I wanted to hear it.''

"Is that why you teach on the side?''

"You been readin' *my* file?''

"Gossip.''

He nodded. ''No, that's not why I teach. I teach because I enjoy it. Most of my students are officers already and they're trying to climb an extra rung on the promotion ladder or they just want to learn. They're motivated.''

"Would you ever quit the force and teach full-time?''

"Actually, I've been thinking about doing that very thing.''

"Why is that?''

He met Risa's gaze. ''Because I'm too damn old to do this anymore. I've seen it all and done it twice. I'm ready to move on.''

GRADY SUDDENLY LEANED forward and grabbed the dash. ''Start the car,'' he ordered. ''The garage door's opening and she's backing out.''

Looking at the Rowling house, Risa did as Grady instructed. The van headed away from them and Risa put her Toyota in gear.

"Not too close," Grady cautioned.

"I know how to tail. I'm very good at it, in fact." Her voice went sharp. "When was the last time you followed a suspect?"

"All right, all right. I get your point." He made an impatient motion with his hand. "Just keep her in sight and don't let her know we're back here."

Rolling her eyes in response, Risa slowed the Toyota while ahead of them, Melinda slid the blue Windstar through a stop sign. When the van swung into the parking lot of a day-care center twenty minutes later, Grady glanced at Risa with new appreciation.

"You *are* good," he said. "I'm impressed."

She sent him a look. "I shoot even better than I drive."

He opened his mouth to answer, but Risa interrupted, nodding toward the center. "She's dropping the kid off. Does she have a job?"

"Not that I know of," he answered. "She didn't before the shooting."

They watched the woman and child join the parade of parents and youngsters going into the low, square building.

Risa didn't look at Grady as she spoke. "You and your wife didn't have children?"

"No."

Her head turned of its own accord.

Grady glanced at her then sighed. "She never

thought the time was right and I didn't push her."
He paused. "I think I knew deep down the marriage
wasn't going to work. I didn't see the point in having
children just so you could fight over them later."

His answer made sense, and it confirmed what
she'd already begun to suspect. Grady was one of
those rare men who really did care more about the
people around him than he did about himself.

They sat in silence until Melinda Rowling reappeared. She walked quickly to her van and climbed
inside, but she didn't pull out of her parking space.
Risa watched as Melinda's head ducked down and
she reached for something on the floorboard. A second later, she came back up then leaned toward the
rearview mirror.

Grady spoke impatiently, squirming in his seat to
get a better look. "What in the hell is she doing?
Getting a phone or—"

"She's putting on lipstick," Risa said calmly. "In
a minute, she'll probably take out some mascara and
a hairbrush, too. She bent down to get her purse."

Finally the van backed out. Risa followed the vehicle to the nearest freeway entrance. Melinda led
them straight into the Village. An upscale area of
shops and older homes near Rice University, the
minivan stood out among the BMWs and Mercedes
SUVs. She slid into the first parking spot she found
and left Risa and Grady stranded.

Grady spoke as he opened the car door. "I'll follow her. You park. We'll reconnect by phone."

She had to go over two more streets until she found an empty slot. Her phone rang as she was locking the car.

"She went into a Cuban place," Grady said. "Lots of windows, though. I'm across the street at a juice bar and I can see her."

Risa hurried down the sidewalk, joining Grady a few minutes later. He'd bought two drinks and was sitting at a bistro table that fronted the street.

"Here." He pushed one of the cups toward her and made a face. "I don't know why the hell they say these things are good for you. They taste like crap."

"Of course they do." Risa climbed onto the stool beside him and reached for the cup. "If they tasted good, they'd be bad for you. That's the way the world works. We always want what we shouldn't have."

Their eyes met over the drinks then they both looked away.

Ten minutes later, Kurt Trundle walked into the restaurant and sat down with Melinda Rowling.

RISA SUCKED IN her breath as Grady cursed.

Kurt Trundle reached over and covered the grieving widow's hand with both of his. Leaning closer,

he said something and she gave him a small smile,
ducking her head and looking up at him through her
lashes. Shades of Princess Diana, Grady groaned.
How long had she been practicing that move?

"Shit," Grady said.

The waitress set drinks before Trundle and Melinda and they lifted their glasses and tapped the rims
together.

Risa spoke with barely disguised excitement in her
voice. "They're celebrating something."

He sent her a look. "C'mon, Risa, you're too good
a cop to jump to conclusions. We don't know that's
what they're doing."

"Oh, for God's sake, there's no other reason to do
what they just did."

"It still doesn't make them killers."

They sat for another hour and watched Trundle
and Melinda eat their lunch. Grady ordered another
round of juice, but the second ones tasted worse than
the first.

Finally Trundle signaled the waitress for their
check and five minutes later he and Melinda were on
the sidewalk. He wrapped her in a tight hug then
pulled back to lightly stroke her cheek. After a bit,
he kissed her and they separated.

Grady stood. "Tell me where you parked and I'll
go get the car while you can watch 'em. We'll meet
at the corner."

Risa fished her keys from her purse and handed them over, giving him directions at the same time. Five minutes later, he pulled to the curb and she jumped in.

"Melinda left and went back toward the freeway. He's just pulling out."

"We'll go with him this time."

"Okay." She nodded toward a dark boxy SUV. "He's up there. In the Hummer. I guess the SWAT guys get paid pretty well, huh?"

"Not that well. He's a car nut—last count, he had six stickers for six vehicles." Grady angled the Toyota back into the line of traffic and they ended up two lengths behind Trundle. "His family has money. Haven't you ever heard of Trundle Towers over at the medical center?"

Grady could feel her stare of surprise. "He's one of *those* Trundles? I'm impressed."

"You should be. Trundle's parents are at every A-list event given in Houston. If they aren't, then it isn't an A-list event."

Her expression turned skeptical.

"I keep up with the society pages," he explained. "His grandfather makes the money and his father gives it away. They're very big in the conservative wing of things. Very big as in White House big. They're very generous with their wealth, too."

"So how on earth did Kurt end up a SWAT cop?"

"That's one for the shrinks, not me." Grady slowed and changed lanes. Trundle was heading for the west side of town. "He doesn't need the money, that's for sure. His house is paid off, he doesn't use credit cards and, as far as I know, he's the only guy on the SWAT team who has his T-shirts tailored."

"You didn't get *that* information from the *Chronicle.*"

Grady threw her a look, then changed lanes again. Trundle was weaving from one side of the freeway to the other, looking for breaks in the traffic. Grady might have thought the cop had spotted them, but almost everyone in Houston drove the same way.

They followed Trundle for another twenty minutes before he took an exit at the last minute.

"He's going to the club." Risa thumped her fist against the dash. "Dammit, I should have realized that's where he was headed when he started out this way."

He glanced across the seat. "The club?"

"Trundle belongs to the same shooting club I do. It's right down here."

The SWAT cop signaled a turn a few miles later then swung the lumbering vehicle into a paved parking lot.

Grady continued past the low-rise building, pulling into the parking lot of a McDonald's a few blocks down to make a U-turn.

Five minutes later they were back on the freeway. Grady tried to make conversation but Risa only answered with grunts. When he parked the Toyota in his driveway, she roused herself from her thoughts and told him goodbye, but her mind was a thousand miles away.

RISA WENT TO BED thinking of Grady and woke up the next morning doing the same thing. The hours in between had probably been filled with dreams of him, too, but she couldn't remember, thank goodness. Being with him yesterday had been enough of a nightmare. She would want to pull him to her and never let go then she'd remember his words and hold herself back. A few minutes later, he'd look at her a certain way or turn his head just so, and the cycle of desire and longing would start all over again. She'd thought the day would never end, but when it did she'd hated to leave him.

The only way she could function was to deliberately focus on the man she'd seen approaching Kurt Trundle in the parking lot of the range as they'd driven past.

The manager of the crime lab, Lawton Calvin, had appeared to be furious as he'd walked up to the SWAT cop, who'd looked none too pleased himself. Risa had said nothing about what she'd seen to Grady and she rationalized her silence to herself that

morning as she headed into work. Grady hadn't told
her he had the tape, so she hadn't told him she'd
spotted the two men. Her actions didn't make sense,
but it did make them even. Maybe she'd tell him
later. After she talked to Calvin.

Stepping out of the elevator, she started to her cubicle on automatic pilot. Suddenly a woman came
out of one of the side offices and Risa had to dodge
to her right to miss her. The other woman did the
same and they stopped just short of colliding. Risa
raised her head with a smile, then her expression
slowly changed. Too late to pretend they were
strangers, she and Lucy stood face-to-face in the center of the corridor.

They said each other's names in tandem, and a
pang of loneliness hit Risa squarely in the chest. It
didn't matter that the hallway was full of people—
all she could think about was how much she'd
missed her friends and the support they'd once given
her.

Lucy recovered first, but her manner was stiff and
uneasy. "Hey, Risa. How are things going?"

"I'm great," she lied. "How're you?"

"Okay, I guess." Lucy's eyes darted over Risa's
shoulder then came back to her face. Lucy didn't
want anyone to see them talking. She would have cut
and run if she could have done so without looking

crazy. "I've been busy, you know. With work and everything."

"Have you seen any of the gang?" The question popped out before Risa could stop it.

"They're all fine." A dull blush spread up Lucy's strong cheekbones. They'd gotten together, Risa realized instantly, and they'd left her out. Although it was no surprise, the discovery hurt, and Risa pulled back. This wasn't high school, she reminded herself. This was the real world, and she had to stand on her own two feet.

She didn't let her reaction show. "That's good," she said calmly.

A clumsy silence filled the space between them, then they both spoke again.

"I've got to get going—"

"I'd better get back—"

They smiled at their awkward synchronicity, then Risa stepped to one side and Lucy started past her. As the other woman drew near, however, Risa had a sudden brainstorm. Before she could decide if it was a good idea or not, she reached out and touched Lucy's arm.

"Luce? Can I...can I ask you something before you go?"

Lucy sent another quick look up and down the corridor.

"I don't really have the time—"

Risa didn't wait for her to finish her excuse. "Do you know a SWAT cop named Kurt Trundle? He's blond, nice looking, blue eyes—"

Lucy nodded almost instantly. "I know *who* he is, but I don't really know him. He was friends with an admin assistant I know named Stacy Brinks. They used to meet sometimes after work for a drink…or, knowing Stacy, for three or four drinks."

"Big boozer?"

"Stacy was. In fact I'm sure I wouldn't have known anything about the situation at all, except we were at a party and the alcohol had been flowing pretty freely. Otherwise, Stacy was very discreet, even with me, and we were pretty close." She paused. "Long story short, I think they might have had something going on, but you know how tough it is around here if you're not part of the 'team.' In the end, Trundle was interested in a long-term relationship and Stacy wasn't. Trundle apparently turned kinda scary after that." Her expression shifted. "Look, Risa, I've really got to go. I'll…see you around, okay?"

Risa wondered why Stacy Brinks was not part of the team, but Lucy was already halfway down the hall. Risa decided she'd just have to find out on her own. And she would. Right after she talked to Lawton Calvin.

THE USUAL STACK of bullshit announcements and memos waited for Grady on the corner of his desk that morning. He swept them into his wastebasket without a second glance, setting his briefcase in their spot. After flipping on his computer, he went for coffee then returned to look up Trundle's personal file. Thoughts of Risa kept intruding, however. Grady knew he should keep his hands off her, but he wasn't sure he had the willpower, despite sending her away the other day. A relationship between the two of them wouldn't take either one of them any way but down. He didn't give a damn for himself, but this wasn't just about him.

Her explanation of what her career meant to her had made him ache, but it took that kind of dedication to be the kind of cop she was. He knew because he'd been one once. Sacrifices were made to reach that level, but what Risa didn't yet understand was that in the end, the rewards weren't always worth what you gave up. She still thought she could make a difference. Naivete aside, if that's what she wanted, then he needed to see that she got the chance. And that meant keeping her out of his bed, no matter how desperately he wanted her there. He'd done a lot of bad things in his life, but ruining a good cop's career wasn't going to be added to the list.

Sipping his coffee, Grady turned his concentration to the task at hand, renewing his memory with the mundane: Trundle's address, his record of commendations, his length of service, complaints against him.

The scant details of the SWAT cop's personal life held none of the messiness inherent in the majority of records that Grady read. He'd never been divorced because he'd never been married and on paper, at least, he seemed like the model citizen. The cleanliness of the man's life said a lot, though. And Grady wasn't sure it was all good.

His coffee was cold by the time he closed the file, exited the program and made his plan. Picking up the phone, he got the information he needed in order to proceed.

He'd let everything slide when he'd started on Risa's investigation and his normally well organized files had become chaotic. He cleaned them up, but while he did so, his mind returned to his living room and Risa.

The time went swiftly. Glancing at his watch, he realized he was running late. He put himself in high gear and reached the Volvo in record time.

Stabbing his remote in the direction of the car, he pressed the button with a jerk, but the click he usually heard didn't happen. He hit the button again, but this time the car locked itself. Frowning, he leaned down and looked through the window. The car had been unlocked already.

"What the hell..." Unlocking the vehicle once more, Grady bent to peer inside and spotted a piece of paper lying on the passenger seat. It had writing on it. And it wasn't his.

Grady set his briefcase down, considered a booby trap, then reached for the door. It opened with a loud snick—no bomb—and Grady reached inside, pulling the note toward him with the end of his ballpoint pen. The letters were all caps, neatly printed in a single line on an ordinary piece of white paper.

SINCE WHEN DO BAD COPS DO THEIR OWN INVESTIGATIONS? BACK OFF, ASSHOLE. SHE'S NOT WORTH IT.

Grady read the note a second time. Then a third. After the fourth, he knew he didn't need a detective to figure this one out.

Somehow, Trundle had learned about Grady and Risa. If they persisted, he'd see that everyone else knew about them, too. And he'd have their jobs.

Crouched beside his open car door, Grady sighed and rocked back on his heels. He hadn't bothered to tell Risa what an asshole Kurt Trundle was because there had been no reason to, but a friend of Grady's had tangled with the SWAT cop before on an excessive force complaint. The IA officer had recommended an extended leave and psychological counseling. Trundle had gotten a slap on the wrist and back pay.

Grady threw his briefcase onto the seat of the car, then closed the door, making sure this time that he locked it. Reaching the ground floor of the parking garage, he started walking.

CHAPTER FOURTEEN

THE EVENING SUN HAD DIPPED behind the high-rise buildings that lined the downtown Houston streets, but the temperature hadn't abated with its disappearance. The unlucky workers who were just now escaping their desks moved down the sidewalks with such lethargy Grady almost slowed himself. Then he remembered his goal and sped up.

Two blocks over and three blocks down, he came to the double doors he'd been searching for, "Roxie's" spelled out on the glass in elaborate gold lettering that seemed inappropriately ornate.

Primarily a boxing gym, Roxie's had been a Houston institution for years. Grady hadn't been too surprised to see the automatic draft from Trundle's paycheck even though he might have expected the SWAT cop to exercise at some expensive fancy-dancy herbal-tea kind of place over by the Galleria and not a sweatshop like Roxie's. The gym probably had the same draw for him that it did for all the cops, Grady decided. It was convenient to downtown and they couldn't get a better deal anywhere else because the owner gave them discounts on their membership. Cops had always worked out here. In his younger years, Grady had been one of them, but it'd been a while since he'd been inside the gym. When he'd called, Roxie had remembered him, though, and had been more than happy to tell him when Trundle worked out. Grady wondered now if Roxie's helpful attitude had been part of Trundle's plan. The SWAT cop obviously wanted to make his stance known.

Grady pushed his way through the doors. The smell of old sweat and testosterone almost knocked him to his knees, the sounds of grunts and groans following up with a hard right. He blinked, then narrowed his eyes, searching the various stations for the trim, blond cop.

"Looking for somebody?"

Grady turned. A young man with stiff hair and a blank look stood right behind him. Under his painted-on Lycra was a body that had been sculpted into rock. Grady eyed him carefully then his ego decided he could probably take him down—the kid had muscles, but he obviously didn't know how to use them. He was eye candy, Grady thought unexpectedly, his ex-wife's term popping into his mind. She'd used the description to label the gay models in New York. He'd told her it wasn't P.C. and she'd told him to go to hell.

"I'm supposed to meet a guy here," Grady answered.

"Does this guy have a name?" The twenty-something's words sounded flirtatious, but Grady told himself he was imagining things.

"Yeah, he does. It's Kurt Trundle."

He couldn't have flipped a switch and gotten a more dramatic change. The blonde stepped back, his expression closing as he pointed toward the rear of the building. "He's in one of the boxing rings. Head back there and you'll find him."

Glancing in the direction he'd pointed, Grady turned back to say thank-you, but the young man was already walking away. As Grady watched, he shot an anxious look over his shoulder then increased his pace until he was practically running.

Dismissing the guy, Grady headed for the rear of the building. As he neared the three rings set up along the back wall, he easily picked out Trundle. A large crowd had gathered around the ropes to watch him box a man who looked to be at least five years younger than himself. Grady realized he had to correct himself. *Boxing* wasn't the right word for what Trundle was doing.

He was beating the poor kid to death and clearly enjoying it. Grady could have arrested him for assault. But he didn't.

A bell sounded and Trundle pulled back from his

opponent, flinging the guy's arms off his shoulders.
Trundle had been his only support and when he with-
drew, the kid crumpled to the canvas, bounced once,
then lay without moving. Spitting out his mouth-
piece, the SWAT cop laughed and high-fived his way
around the ropes until he came to where Grady
waited. There was no surprise in his eyes. In fact,
confirming Grady's suspicions, Trundle actually
looked pleased to see him.

Grady nodded toward the center of the ring. An
employee of the gym had gotten the still-dopey
fighter on his feet and was trying to get him to the
corner.

"I'm real impressed, Trundle. That was quite an
exhibition."

Trundle raised his right hand to his mouth and
tugged at the laces of his gloves with his teeth. He
loosened them and spoke. "What are you doing here,
Wilson? Roxie's isn't your kind of place."

"It isn't," Grady answered. "But neither is the
Village Smoothie Shoppe and I sat there for an hour
just so I could watch you and Melinda Rowling eat
lunch across the street."

If the blond cop was surprised at Grady's direct-
ness, he hid it.

"Don't you have better things to do than be a
Peeping Tom? Maybe you and your girlfriend need
to go back to church." He smiled sweetly. "Al-

though I must say, you two don't exactly worship like anyone I've ever seen.''

Trundle had seen Grady and Risa at Saint John's that day downtown. The revelation left Grady feeling queasy, but at least he knew they hadn't been spotted when they'd trailed Trundle—he would have said something, if he had.

"I'm not sure I know what you mean.'' Grady pursed his lips thoughtfully. ''You wanna be more specific there?''

"You know exactly what I mean.''

"Hey, I'm just an IA cop.'' Grady draped his hands over the bottom rope of the ring. ''You have to explain certain things in detail to us or we don't get them.'' He paused. ''You know, things like why you seem to have such a close relationship with Melinda Rowling. Can you explain that to me?''

"I've been comforting her,'' he said easily. ''She's grief-stricken.''

Grady pursed his lips. ''She doesn't seem too stricken to me. At least not with grief. Maybe pills...''

Trundle ignored the reference. ''She covers up her distress well.''

"And just how long have you been comforting her? Would that have started before her husband died?''

Without taking his eyes from Grady's, Trundle let

his right glove drop to the canvas where it landed with a dull thud. "That wouldn't make sense, would it? For me to comfort her before she needed it."

"Lots of things don't make sense." Grady shrugged. "Look at poor ol' Luke Rowling. Cut down in the prime of his life." Grady shook his head. "Just doesn't seem right and here you are, with his wife already..."

Trundle stilled. "If I were you, I'd back off and find somebody else to hassle. Warnings are warnings for a reason. Next time things might not be so simple."

Amazed at the man's arrogance, Grady shook his head. "That sounds like a threat to me, Trundle. I'd hate to have to write you up for being uncooperative with an IA investigation. You know that won't look good on the nice clean report card you've got going in your file."

With a look of disgust, Trundle delivered the message he'd brought Grady to the gym to hear.

"Call it whatever you want, Wilson, the facts stay the same. You better watch your back and remember who I am. Your career will go a lot smoother, and so will your girlfriend's."

BY THE TIME Risa got away from her desk that evening, Lawton Calvin had already left. Disappointed but determined, she drove away from headquarters and went directly to her father's house. He didn't seem as surprised to see her as he had been the previous time, but his eyes rounded all the same when he opened his door and found her on the sidewalk.

"I've got to ask you something."

"Okay." He opened the door wider and she stepped inside. "You, uh, want something to drink or—"

"I don't have time," she said. "But I need to know more about the case you mentioned the other day, the frame-up you and Bobby investigated."

He'd been frowning, but his face cleared. "Yeah, yeah. Far as I know, Bobby's second cousin never called back on that. But lemme buzz him right now and make sure."

Risa followed him into the kitchen where the same dark green phone hung on the same rose-papered wall that had been there when she'd been a teenager. Her father dialed his ex-partner's number by memory as she stood by and shifted impatiently from one foot to the other.

They spoke in shorthand like old friends do. "No...yeah...yeah, yeah. And that was you know... yeah. He was a mean son of a... Yeah... I'm not sure. You're right. Okay. Thanks."

Her father finished the cryptic conversation too quickly to have learned anything, she decided a moment later. Replacing the receiver, he shook his head and turned to her, confirming her assumption. "The kid never called back, but Bobby finally remembered some of the details. It was a professional hit. The husband wanted the wife dead, but he wanted her lover to look like he'd been the trigger man so he could get rid of both of them at once. This was back in the sixties. Things weren't quite as tight as they are now. They planted some evidence in lover-boy's car then switched what they couldn't plant. It was a big damn mess, but we finally got it straight."

Risa tried not to show her disappointment. She'd been hoping for a revelation. Or maybe a miracle.

"That's it?" she asked.

He looked at her steadily then he pointed to the kitchen table. "You know more than you think you do. Sit down and talk. Tell me what you've learned."

They went over everything again, but in the end, neither one of them could come up with a new angle.

"I just don't understand it," Risa confessed. "I feel like I'm missing something and if I could try just a little bit harder, I'd figure out what it is."

His best advice was for her to think about Lawton Calvin and the crime lab. "The lab's always the weakest link. I think something might be going on there," he said. "I'd look into that a little closer."

Swinging her purse over her shoulder, she stood up and thanked him, then silently discounted his words. Security wasn't perfect at headquarters, but a new generation of cops ran the place now. Switching evidence and beating people up were ghosts from the past. As she started for the front door, his voice stopped her.

"Risa?"

She looked over her shoulder at him. "Yeah?"

He pushed himself up from the table and took a step toward her. His voice sounded strained. "We've had our differences in the past, but you're a damn good cop. Don't let some son of a bitch out there make it seem otherwise. You keep at this until it's resolved."

Her mouth fell open. "I...I don't know what to say."

"Don't say anything." He turned back to the table, gathered up their coffee mugs and carried them to the sink. "Just go home and do what I said."

As a child, she'd thought he was a giant. His back was still broad and straight enough to block the evening sunlight coming through the window about the counter. Ignoring his order to leave, she walked slowly to his side and stared at his profile. "You just called me a damn good cop?"

He turned to face her. Their eyes collided for one swift moment, then he looked away. "So what?" he asked stiffly. "I complimented you. What's the big deal? A father can't say something nice to his daughter once in a while?"

"You've *never* said anything like that before. At least, not to me," she added.

"I had my reasons."

"Yeah, Dad, I know you did. They're named Ed, Phil and Dan. You didn't care what I did as long as they wore the blue."

"You don't know what the hell you're talking about, Risa."

"Then why don't you spell it out?" Fueled by the worry and anxiety of the past few weeks, Risa felt her emotions take control of her mouth. "Why don't you go ahead and tell me exactly why you've never thought I had what it took to be a cop. If I don't know what I'm talking about, then you deserve an Oscar."

He turned to her, his eyes blazing. "I wanted something better for you, okay? I wanted you to have a good job, dammit! Something safe, something important. Something...clean! I didn't want you rolling around in the gutter with drunks like I did for twenty-five years. It was never a matter of whether or not you could handle the work." He stopped and drew a deep breath. "I wanted something better for you. I wanted to...protect you."

Shocked confusion rolled over her in a wave that almost took her under. "But I thought you said—"

"I know what I said," he interrupted. "And I know what you thought."

She stared at him speechlessly while inside her chest, anger squeezed her heart and held it tight, bitterness and disbelief accompanying the reaction. "How could you have done this? It...it's crazy. It's cruel and heartless and—" She broke off, her voice cracking. "For God's sake, Dad, why in the hell didn't you just tell me the truth?"

"Because you wouldn't have listened." His voice was blunt and when their eyes met, she was the one who looked away first. "You're exactly like your mother," he said quietly. "Stubborn as hell. I knew I'd never change your mind if I asked, so I had to try something other than the truth."

Risa's eyes swam, but she blinked away the tears. She'd be damned if she'd cry at this point. "So why are you telling me this now?" she said hoarsely. "Why, after all this time?"

"When the shit hit the fan with Rowling's death, everything changed. You...needed help."

Breaking the silence that followed, she said, "Do you have any idea how much you've hurt me?"

"It was for your own good," he said obstinately. "I thought you'd give up and get a good job. A *decent* job. I...I didn't care if you didn't love me. I just wanted you safe. Maybe it was selfish on my part."

"Selfish? I can't believe—"

He stopped her, gripping the counter with both

hands, a vein throbbing in his neck as he turned to stare at her. "All right! I screwed up. I'm a terrible father! You can blame me for the rest of your life for every little problem you have, okay?"

The kitchen went quiet again.

"I don't think I can forgive this," she said.

"Then don't." His jaw twitched. "But know this—you're a better cop than I ever was and ten times the officer your brothers are. I know now that you'll never leave the force and you probably shouldn't. So go ahead and hate me for the rest of eternity, but whatever you do, don't let the bastard behind this take the life from you. You wouldn't let me do it. Don't let him do it, either."

ROWLING'S WIDOW wouldn't even let Grady inside when he showed up that evening. Unwilling to push her, Grady asked his questions through the screen door and she denied everything from the other side.

"I don't know what you're talking about," she insisted. "I didn't have lunch with Kurt Trundle and even if I had, why would you care? It's still a free world, Mr. Wilson."

He started to correct her—it was Lieutenant Wilson—but she'd already closed the door in his face. Grady walked down the sidewalk, shaking his head.

Driving on automatic, he aimed his car for the freeway. For once, traffic was light. He only wished his thoughts felt the same. The case was getting more and more complicated and he wasn't sure what to do next.

Taking his exit, he drew to a stop at the red light and muttered to himself, his mind switching gears. His intuition told him Trundle was the key, but how? And why? Was there insurance money Grady hadn't yet uncovered? Had Trundle killed Rowling because of the illicit love affair with Melinda? Had Rowling found out and been jealous?

Was Grady on track, or was he in love?

Only when a horn sounded behind him, did he realize the light had changed. He floored the Volvo, turned left and reached his street twenty minutes later. His mind completely focused on his thoughts, he pulled into his driveway and parked.

Risa was waiting on his front porch.

SHE HELD UP her hand before he could speak. "I know you don't want me here, but I need to talk to you."

After leaving her father's, Risa had desperately wanted to call one of her friends, but that wasn't an option so she'd driven to Grady's house, feeling a turmoil that went beyond anger, beyond hurt.

Grady looked as if he wanted to turn her away, but he unlocked his door, flipped on the lights and stepped aside, Risa passing before him.

Their eyes met and he pulled her into his arms. His embrace was nothing like it'd been before. This was gentle and soothing. He kissed her slowly, his mouth making its way around her throat, up her chin and to her lips. Lifting her arms, she wrapped them around his neck and clung to him, swallowing the sting that had been building in her throat ever since she'd talked to her father.

When he pulled away, everything rushed back.

Her words spilled out as he led her into his living room. They sat on the couch and she told him what had happened.

"Son of a bitch." His expression turned fierce as he cursed. "I can't believe he'd do that to you."

"I can," she said quietly. "He's the most obstinate man I've ever known. He said I was like my mother—stubborn—but he got it backward. *He* was always the one who had to have his way." She lifted her eyes to Grady's. "But it doesn't matter. I'm more tenacious than either one of them could ever dream of being."

Grady didn't smile but a light came into his eyes. He lifted a hand to her cheek. "Is that a warning?"

"I'm afraid it is. I saw Lucy this morning and I have to tell you what she said—"

He held up his hand. "Whatever it is, hear this first. Trundle knows about us. He's threatened to tell the brass unless we back off."

She processed his information, a few more pieces of the puzzle slipping into place, her expression turning excited. "This could only mean one thing, Grady. Trundle's behind what happened...he has to be. He and Melinda *must* have engineered Luke's death."

"I'm beginning to believe you. But how in the hell did they do it? And why?"

"I don't know the 'how,' but the 'why' is obvious. They were having an affair."

"That's not good enough. They could have been screwing around, sure, but why kill Luke? I know it's happened, of course, but it just doesn't seem to fit right here. The motivation isn't strong enough."

"What I heard today might make you change your mind." Standing, Risa started to pace. "Lucy knows someone Trundle dated. Her friend said Trundle got really serious really fast. She said he was frightening, he was so insistent. Maybe he fell hard like that for Melinda, too. It's possible, you know."

"Can we talk to Lucy's friend?"

"I've got to find her first. She's an admin assistant named Stacy Brinks. I meant to look her up today and see if she's still on the payroll—"

Grady's expression shifted so drastically that Risa fell silent, her explanation forgotten. Even his eyes seemed to chill, the color switching from dark gray to cold silver. "W-what is it, Grady?"

"Are you talking about the Stacy Brinks down in Records?"

Risa nodded impatiently. "Yes. She and Lucy are friends. I never met the woman but—"

"That's obvious."

"Why?"

"Because Stacy Brinks is not a woman, Risa. Stacy Brinks is a man."

RISA FROZE, her expression locking itself into surprise and disbelief. Finally she blinked and the motion seemed to set her free from shock. "That's impossible! Lucy said—"

"Call her." Grady pulled his cell phone from his pocket and handed it to her. "Make sure we're talking about the same person."

She gripped his phone and dialed. The conversation was short, and Grady could tell by her face, he'd made no mistake. She hit the end button and handed the unit back to him, an emotion too sharp to be called disappointment sweeping over her expression.

"You're right." Her answer was hollow and distant. "We are talking about the same person. Stacy Brinks is a man. And he dated Trundle." She walked to the couch and sat down heavily. "Kurt's gay. I can't believe this. God, we haven't just been on the wrong track, we've been on the wrong damn train!"

The news did put a different spin on things, but

Grady found himself focusing on the pain in Risa's eyes instead of what they'd just learned. Nothing was more important to him than erasing her hurt, and suddenly he knew no matter what happened, when this case was over, so was he.

"What are we going to do?" she asked in a broken voice. "I've worked this thing from every direction possible but every time I think I'm getting somewhere, I run into another wall. I—I don't know what else to do."

"You don't have to do anything." He smoothed a hand over the back of her hair. "That's what I've been trying to tell you all along, Risa. Let me do it. It's my job."

"But—"

He silenced her protest with his mouth, his lips gently covering hers. She responded immediately, almost hungrily, and feeling her need, Grady's own desire grew. He told himself to pull away and turn back. If he had any chance in hell of helping her now, he needed to concentrate on the case itself and not Risa.

But even as he argued with himself, he knew he was past that point. Risa had become more important to him than the case. And right now, she needed comfort.

Deepening his kiss, Grady let his hands drop to her shoulders and then down her back. He slipped his hands beneath her blouse and found bare skin. Everywhere he touched, she was warm and soft. She shouldn't have been that way, he thought in a daze. Risa was the toughest woman he'd ever known, but beneath her armor, that was far from the case.

Pulling his shirt from his pants, she began to unbutton it and a moment later, her lips were pressed against his neck. He reached for her blouse to remove it, but she shook her head. Her eyes locked on his, she stood and slowly undressed herself.

Then she undressed him.

Then she led him to the bedroom.

THE HOUSE WAS SILENT as Risa held Grady's hand and walked in front of him. Inside her chest, her heart was racing so fast she actually felt dizzy. Nothing could have stopped her, though. His embrace offered the only hope she had of maintaining her sanity, the only place of refuge she had left. She needed to be in Grady's arms and she wanted to be in his bed. He could make her forget.

A moment later, that's exactly where they were. She made him stretch out then she straddled him and, starting at the top of his head, she began to kiss him. Slowly, lingeringly. Her lips touched him gently in some places, roughly in others. By the time she got to his waist, his hands were insistent on her shoulders, his need obvious.

She took him into her mouth but only briefly, before continuing down to his toes. When she finished, she started kissing him once more, her mouth and hands working their way upward this time.

She was at the halfway point when he moaned and grabbed her shoulders. Flipping her over to the bed, he began to mimic her actions. She paid for every nip and gentle kiss she'd given him with building agony, his mouth and fingers teasing her. When she thought the end was near, he began again.

Risa lost touch with where she was. Her world was the bed and Grady and nothing else. She cried his name several times and, in the end, she screamed, just as she had the first time.

They fell asleep wrapped in each other's arms.

RISA WOKE in the middle of the night. Grady lay beside her, his hand twisted in her hair.

She gently untangled his fingers, then she slipped out of the bed. She didn't walk away, though. She stood by the edge and stared down at the man who'd become so important to her. She wasn't sure how it had happened, but he'd turned into someone she needed. The idea scared her. She'd never needed anyone but herself before this.

Padding naked into the living room, Risa grabbed the first piece of clothing she found, Grady's shirt. Thrusting her arms through the sleeves, she rolled them up and wandered into the kitchen, her footsteps as random as her thoughts. She filled a glass of water, drank it, then returned to the living room.

If Melinda and Kurt Trundle weren't having an affair, then what *was* going on between the two of them? Risa considered the possibility that Trundle could have been bisexual but she immediately dismissed the idea. Thinking back to the embrace she'd witnessed been Melinda and Trundle, Risa realized something about it had bothered her at the time but she'd put the notion aside and forgotten about it. Now she remembered—and understood. Their actions had held no passion. Trundle was gay. And he was using Melinda's vulnerability to his advantage.

The connection between Melinda and Trundle was still there, but it wasn't configured the way Risa had thought. She found herself standing in front of Grady's television cabinet. Her fingers reached out and she opened the double doors. The tape was right where it'd been when she'd seen it the first time. She caught her breath. Did she really want to put herself through the torture of seeing it again? She had to, she decided after a moment. If there was even the slightest chance she could learn something from viewing the tape one more time, she owed it to herself and to Grady to try.

She punched it into the slot and turned on the set.

The recording picked up a few minutes past where it'd been when Grady had switched it off.

The now-familiar scene of Tequila Jack's parking lot flashed onto the screen, the tarmac full of people and cars. Risa put her hand to her chest as the tape played and she spotted herself sitting on the curb. One medic was kneeling at her side while another one rummaged through a kit nearby. Recalling the moment as if she were still there, her pulse raced painfully.

She remembered exactly what she'd been thinking as the man had cleaned up her wound. She'd been staring at a bullet casing that had landed by the curb. Even in her shock, she'd noted its placement, thinking she had to remember to tell the techs about it later. The metal jacket was barely visible in the frame.

She was absent from the next shot. After that, she watched a variety of officers and crime-scene attendants going over the area.

Samuel Andrews, the lieutenant in charge, dominated the next few pictures. She glanced at the time recording and saw Grady come into focus a little more than an hour after the shooting. He talked to the homicide investigator for a bit, then the frame switched again. The random snapshots that followed didn't amount to much. Nothing but cops and techs swarmed in and out of the picture.

Punching the rewind button, Risa stared numbly as the awful sequences played in reverse, the surreal images flying by—the cops, techs, her figure by the curb, the meds arriving. When she realized the tape had reached the point where she'd see Luke's body again, she seemed to wake up. Her hand shot out to the recorder but, at the last minute, she paused, an officer in black suddenly catching her eye. He wore the clothing of a SWAT team member and, looking closer, she recognized the blond hair and striking features of Kurt Trundle. Her curiosity aroused, she hit the play button and backed up the tape a bit more, checking the timer as she did so.

A tech walked by, then ten minutes later, Kurt passed the curb. In several subsequent frames, Kurt was in some but absent from others. Risa let the video continue until she finally saw her image sitting on the sidewalk again. Her face wore such a stunned expression she wasn't sure she would have recognized herself if she hadn't remembered the moment with such crystalline clarity.

The recollection set something in motion inside her brain. She tried to catch the random flash but the task proved harder than she would have imagined, the slippery thought too elusive to snag. She told herself to concentrate, then as she did, her abstraction turned into confusion.

She rewound the tape until the tech and then Trundle came back into focus. She played the images again, this time in slow motion, her eyes going to the ground instead of to the men themselves. Her pulse stuttered and her body went cold. She had to be mistaken. Once again, she fast-forwarded to the frame that showed her sitting on the curb.

She froze the segment, her nose practically against the television set. Placing her fingers against the screen, Risa held her breath and stared, her mouth open in shock.

Suddenly Grady spoke from behind her. "We were wrong about Melinda." Risa turned dumbly as Grady continued. "But we *were* right about Trundle."

He walked across the room and took her hands. He had on a pair of baggy drawstring pants and no shirt, and when he squeezed her fingers, she hardly felt his touch.

"I started thinking about something when I woke up," he said. "So I went and checked my files. Gay or straight, I think Trundle killed Luke Rowling and set you up for it. And I just figured out why."

"That's good," Risa said, her heart leaping into her throat as her paralysis finally broke. "Because I think I just figured out how."

CHAPTER FIFTEEN

HIS EYES WENT WIDE, then darkened. "You first," Grady commanded.

Risa pointed to the television set. "Come watch."

She played the segment of the tape showing the tech and then Trundle. Then she went to the frame where she sat on the curb. Grady stared and shook his head when she stopped the recorder.

"Look again," she instructed. "Look for what *isn't* there."

She replayed the tape and pointed to the curb as the tech walked by. Then Trundle came and went. Finally, when Risa's image showed up, she pointed to the curb again.

"There's a casing by my foot," she said quietly. "It *wasn't* there when the tech walked by the first time or he would have stopped and marked it or even bagged it. No one walks by that spot again except Trundle." She turned her eyes to Grady's. "But the casing was there when I sat down later. I remember seeing it."

At her words, Grady blinked, a stunned look coming over his face. She didn't need to ask if he understood; it was clear he did.

"I told you I had thirteen rounds in my weapon and that I shot seven times, but you said eight casings were found." She tapped the glass screen and it made a hollow sound. "That's why. Right *there* is where the eighth casing came from. Trundle planted it."

"What about the round missing from your pistol?"

She clenched her jaw. "I'd risk next year's salary that Lawton Calvin got rid of it after I turned my .44 in to the lab for testing."

"Why would the manager of the crime lab do something like that?"

"I don't know, but he and Trundle are connected." She explained seeing the two men together.

"And the slug that killed Luke?"

"I *can't* explain that either," she admitted. "But I know I didn't kill him. Either ballistics screwed up the match—which is doubtful—or the slug the coroner recovered wasn't the same slug that ballistics got to test and compare."

"You think it could have been switched?"

"It's an option. My dad and I talked earlier about one of his old cases where something similar happened and it made me wonder. Things aren't as tight in the lab as they're made out to be and Calvin has to be part of the problem. It's a wild-eyed guess, but I'd say Trundle's either paying him off or blackmailing him.''

"That would fit," Grady said. "Especially when you combine it with the information I went to check on. I had the rap sheet for Sanchez, the second shooter, in my files. I wanted to make sure before I said anything to you, but I was right.''

"About what?''

"Sanchez and his buddy were picked up in a SWAT team operation a few months ago, but they were released without charges. Trundle was the officer in charge. He let them go.''

"Why?''

"I think he was already planning something and needed them. In his eyes, they were disposable. He knew whatever happened to them later wouldn't matter.''

The image of the two men stumbling out of the club sent something skittering up her back. Then she remembered. "They weren't really drunk," she said. "I wondered about it at the time, then I forgot.'' Risa's stomach turned at the thought. "He knew I'd shoot them.''

"Sure, he did. Hell, I wouldn't be surprised if he gave them blanks. The techs never found any slugs that night but yours.''

"Why?" Her voice cracked. "Why would he do this?"

"It all comes down to motivation. Every time. I've been going crazy trying to figure out how Trundle and Melinda would profit from Luke's death, then I realized where I'd gone wrong when we learned he's gay. I've been looking at things from the wrong end of the binoculars. I shouldn't have concentrated on what Trundle stood to *gain*. I should have looked at what Trundle has to *lose*." He paused. "The man is set to receive a fortune. What if the elder members of his oh-so-perfect family aren't as open-minded as the rest of us? What if he won't get his inheritance if the truth came out? Maybe Melinda's his beard."

"But what does any of that have to do with Luke?"

"Maybe Rowling knew. Could he have been blackmailing Trundle?"

"That doesn't sound like the Luke I knew." Risa hesitated. "Then again, Luke wasn't himself those last few weeks. I guess anything's possible."

"I'm not sure, either, but with that tape—" Grady nodded toward the VCR "—and a good judge, we've got enough for a search warrant."

RISA TURNED to Grady and moved a step closer, wrapping her arms around his waist. "You finally believe I'm innocent, don't you?"

"I thought you were all along," he replied. "But thinking alone won't get you too far in this job. I had to have evidence, Risa, and you know that."

He lifted her chin with his fingers then bent down to kiss her. For a second, her lips trembled beneath his, then she gathered herself and kissed him back, her arms holding him tight. Grady wanted to pick her up and carry her to his bedroom and make them both forget the reasons they'd come together, but he couldn't do that. Not now. Maybe when this was over, they could have some kind of future, but what that was, he had no idea.

Regardless, he allowed himself a few minutes to fantasize along those lines, then he gently untangled her arms from his waist. "We have to get to headquarters," he said. "I want to put an APB out on Trundle and get the warrant going."

THEY WERE ALMOST to the front door when Grady stopped abruptly. "Damn! I've got to get my briefcase," he said. "It's in the study. Give me a second."

"I'll wait in the car." Risa tilted her head toward the street. "Don't take too long."

He nodded and started toward the back of the house as Risa opened the front door and went outside. The sticky night air was hot and expectant, and a lingering heaviness in it felt ominous. Risa scoffed at the idea as soon as it entered her mind, but after the day she'd had, who could blame her? She took two steps and tried to clear her mind.

Without warning, a hand clamped over her mouth and a pistol dug into her ribs. The voice in her ear was harsh but familiar. Fear lurched through her as Kurt Trundle spoke.

"Pull your weapon from its holster and hand it to me, barrel first."

She did exactly as he ordered and she felt his movements as he took her Glock and put it in his waistband. "Good. Now don't do anything but reverse your steps. If you try to scream, I'll shoot him before he clears the door."

Her heart pounded.

"Do you understand me?" His breath smelled like peppermints.

She nodded.

"All right. We're walking to the door as if you forgot something, then we're going inside."

He forced her backward, a shadow on the porch no one could have seen even if they looked. "Open the door," he said. "Slowly."

Her nervous fingers slipped against the round brass knob then found purchase. She turned it and the door gave way. Trundle waited a second longer then they pushed inside together. Grady hadn't had time to return and for half a second, Risa thought she might have a chance. Her eyes darted frantically around the entry as she looked for something she could kick over or knock down. All she saw was Trundle's steady stare as it met hers in the wall mirror.

"Don't even think about it," he whispered. "You know what kind of shot I am. He wouldn't have a chance."

Risa nodded again, and Trundle dragged her into the living room. Before leaving the room, Grady had switched off the lights and only the blue glow of the blank television screen remained. The color painted the furniture and walls with an underwater tint. Trundle laid Risa's gun on a table beside the wall then suddenly jerked her to him.

Against her back, he tensed, tightening his arm around her neck. "Not a word," he breathed.

A second later she heard Grady walking toward the front door. He opened it and stepped outside. The lock turned and his footsteps rang out as he headed toward the street, the sound fading after a moment.

Trundle loosened his hold a fraction.

"He's going to come back when he doesn't find me," Risa said quietly.

"That's all right," Trundle answered. "By then, you'll be dead. And he'll be next."

CAREFULLY SEARCHING left and right, Grady paused on the sidewalk, then headed for his car. He unlocked the driver's-side door and climbed inside, then turned around once more and craned his neck, eyeing the sidewalk and the street behind him as if looking for Risa. When the map light went out, he reached up and switched the lamp all the way off, his heart pounding so loud in the silence he imagined the neighbors could hear it.

Grady had installed a burglar alarm a few years back when a cop he'd investigated had gotten upset over an unfavorable report. Officially, the officer had threatened "bodily harm." Unofficially, he'd promised Grady he was going to find out where he lived then come over and break both his "friggin' arms."

Whenever a door or window opened, whether the system was armed or not, a light blinked on a panel in his bedroom. After going to his study, he'd seen the green dot pulsing. He'd started to call out for Risa then he'd decided against it. He had a security camera hidden on the front porch and a real time monitor, too. His legs had turned to water as he'd stared at the flickering screen.

Climbing to the other side of the vehicle, Grady opened the door and slid out. He had two, maybe three minutes, certainly no more than five.

Using the cover of Risa's Toyota, he eased another fifteen feet. Just behind her Camry, his neighbor had parked his camper, and for once, Grady was grateful. He sprinted the length of the Winnebago, then dashed between the houses to the street south of his own.

Snaking through the darkened alleys, he doubled around until he came to his own backyard. Climbing over the cedar fence, he approached the rear of the house in silence, his hand on his weapon. Within a minute, he stood beside the window in his living room. Taking a deep breath, he eased his body beneath the brick ledge then slowly raised his head to peer inside.

What he saw turned his blood to ice.

"I DON'T KNOW what you think you're doing, Trundle, but whatever it is, you aren't going to succeed."

Forcing her into a nearby chair, Trundle pushed Risa down as she spoke. He held both of her hands behind her back and gave them a painful yank. "Shut up," he said. "I don't need your commentary. Especially since it's wrong."

She heard the distinctive snick of plastic handcuffs. Trundle tightened them more than was necessary and the hard edges bit into the skin around her wrists. He came back around and faced her.

"You and your IA man have been so wrong all along it's almost laughable. I'm not worried."

"You should be." She spoke with an assurance she didn't feel. "We know Lawton Calvin's been working with you and we know you killed the second shooter.''

He turned his blue eyes on hers.

"We also know your affair with Melinda Rowling isn't real.''

He blinked this time but recovered quickly. "That leaves quite a bit you *don't* know, doesn't it?"

"The rest doesn't matter," she answered. "We've got enough on you right now to send you to Huntsville. I've heard they love ex-cops at The Walls.''

The name of the death-row prison didn't appear to faze him.

"You and your buddy aren't going to send me anywhere because I'm sending both of you to hell first.'' He shook his head in a parody of dejection. "A murder-suicide...so sad. Often happens with burned-out cops. Guess you just couldn't take the pressure.''

Risa's dry mouth made it hard to talk but she persisted. Once Grady came through that door—and he would any moment—he was a dead man.

"I think *you're* the one who couldn't take the pressure," she answered. "I just don't understand what Luke had to do with any of it. He was a damn good cop and you killed him. Why?''

Trundle's expression morphed slowly from puzzlement to wonder to bitterness as he stared at her in the blue light. He cursed softly then shook his head.

"You didn't know, did you? He told me that you knew, but he lied about that, too, the son of a bitch. I can't believe this. And I trusted him." He cursed again, but his expression didn't match his words. No anger or rancor crossed his face, only something that looked surprisingly like regret.

His reaction made no sense then something seemed to unwind inside Risa. She held her breath, then expelled it slowly, the whole picture coming together for the first time since Luke had died. His attitude toward her, his words that night, Melinda's actions...no wonder she'd gone nuts over Grady's questions about "an affair" in the family. *She* hadn't been the one cheating.

Melinda had never been Kurt Trundle's lover.

Luke had.

She should have been more shocked, but Risa had gone past that point. "You didn't have to kill him," she said sadly.

"Yes, I did." Trundle's face hardened. "He wouldn't leave Melinda. I couldn't let her have him."

"That's crazy."

"Yes," he replied. "It probably is, but that's how love works sometimes."

HOLDING HIS WEAPON against his chest, Grady stood in the darkness of the dining room and listened.

When he'd looked through the window and seen Risa tied up, cold determination had replaced his earlier concern. He'd thought Trundle was smarter than this, but obviously his desperation was too big to contain.

Staying as close as possible to the wall, Grady crept toward the living room. He waited only a second, then he swung around the corner and extended his weapon.

"Drop the gun and move away," he said loudly. "Do it right now, Trundle, or I swear to God, I'll shoot you."

RISA'S HEART FLEW into her throat.

She'd been praying Grady would simply leave when he couldn't find her, but deep down, she'd known he'd return. Thank God, he'd somehow realized what was going on and Trundle hadn't been able to surprise him.

After a momentary start, Trundle answered, "I'm not dropping anything, Wilson. What do you think this is, *Law and Order*? I'm going to kill her and then I'm going kill you and after that, I'm going to have a drink and celebrate."

"I've called for backup," Grady said in a calm voice. "Your SWAT buddies are going to be surrounding the house any minute. Let's not make this situation any crazier than it already is."

"You're the one who got us here. If you'd left

everything alone, the situation wouldn't have developed."

"I'm not paid to leave things alone," Grady answered. "I'm paid to find out the truth." His eyes flickered to Risa's. "Are you all right?"

Trundle answered for Risa. "She's fine. But she won't be for long, and neither will you."

Taking a step to his right, Grady ignored the threat. "You won't get away with this."

"Yes, I will," the other man replied. "Have you forgotten that my last name is Trundle? It's a name that goes a long way here in Houston, Wilson. There might be a little stink at first, but the press will quickly forget. Money makes bad things go away."

"How much of that money is gonna be yours when your family finds out about your lifestyle?"

"They aren't going to," he said confidently. "I've got a girlfriend, remember? We're quite close."

Risa closed her eyes and held back a groan. Poor Melinda. First Luke, now this. Thinking she'd been the one to keep Luke from him, Trundle had obviously set out to destroy her.

Grady moved another step to his right. "I somehow doubt that relationship will last. Once she finds out you engineered her husband's death, Melinda Rowling won't be too pleased."

"I didn't engineer shit. I killed Luke with a single shot from fifty yards away." He looked down at

Risa. "I forgot to warn Sanchez and his buddy how good a shooter you are, not that it mattered since I provided them with the guns…and the blanks. I apologized when I visited Ricardo the other night. I let him know I was sorry his print card got lost, too."

"And ballistics?" Grady asked.

"Calvin hasn't been very discreet with a small problem he's got. He likes little children. I offered to see that he gets help with his situation, but he declined and in return for my silence, he substituted the slug from Luke's body with one I provided. Ballistics analyzed the one they were given. Unfortunately for Risa, the one they analyzed came from her gun."

He was proud of what he'd managed to do and eager to brag. So eager, Risa finally realized, he hadn't noticed how close Grady had gotten to the two of them.

GRADY TENSED. He was ten feet away, maybe less, from the chair where Risa was tied. He could leap that far and fall on top of her, but he'd have to shoot Trundle in midair. Risa could have done it, but Grady wasn't sure he could. Grady weighed his choices as Trundle continued to talk, then it hit him. The SWAT cop didn't own all the odds. They had something to negotiate with, too.

"You planned the whole thing quite well, Trundle.

I'll give you that." Grady sent a steady look to Risa then turned his eyes back to the cop. "You skipped one detail, though. Unfortunately, for *you*," he said mockingly, "we have proof of what you did. There was a security cam in the parking lot. It recorded everything."

A look of alarm crossed Trundle's face then it cleared immediately. "I was too far away when I shot. Don't even try—"

"I'm not talking about the shooting," Grady said. "I'm talking about the fake evidence you planted."

"You're bullshitting me."

"There's a copy in the VCR right behind you. Go ahead and watch it."

Trundle's gaze flicked toward the television. The blue light was steady and the color matched his eyes.

"We were looking at it right before you got here. That's why the TV's on." Grady motioned with his gun. "Go ahead. Be my guest."

"You turn it on," Trundle ordered.

"I'd be happy to," Grady replied. "But first you're going to untie Risa and let her go. If you don't, you'll never find out where the original tape is."

For the first time, he seemed to hesitate.

Grady pressed his case. "Believe me, Trundle, it *will* be found. And you *will* be caught. Unless you cut her loose."

"Then what?"

"We'll decide that together. It'll depend on you," Grady promised.

"How do I know you won't screw me?"

Grady smiled unpleasantly. "How do you think I've managed to survive this long in IA, Trundle? Where do you think the Porsche came from? The clothes? The house..." He shook his head. "Look at it like this, you've got extra income from your family, and so do I. HPD's just one big happy family, right? Most of the cops I've investigated have been more than happy to help me...when I've helped them."

Believing Grady was dirty was easy for Trundle since that was the side he walked on. He thought a moment longer, then he reached inside his pocket, pulled out a small knife and tossed it to the floor at Risa's feet.

"Pick it up," he told Grady, "and slice her cuffs." He pointed the gun at Risa's head. "You do anything but move your butt to the couch, and he's a dead man. You understand?"

Risa nodded, her eyes dark as she turned to Grady. Kneeling at her feet, he picked up the pocketknife then moved behind her chair, his weapon on Kurt the whole time. When Grady glanced down to look for a place to cut, Risa whispered urgently.

"Drop your gun and dive right," she ordered. "I'll grab it and go left."

CHAPTER SIXTEEN

RISA WENT ONE WAY and Grady went the other.
Trundle screamed a curse and fired a half second
later, but Risa shot back. He grabbed his shoulder
and cried out, tumbling to the carpet, his pistol hitting the floor first then bouncing to one side. Risa
launched herself to where the gun landed and covered it with her body. Wrapping her fingers around
the grip, she scooted backward and aimed at the same
time, a weapon in each hand.

Trundle lay motionless. Risa jumped to her feet
and called to Grady without looking. "Are you
okay?"

He didn't answer.

She chanced a look and wished she hadn't.

Grady was slumped against a chair, one side of his
face covered in blood, his hands lying limply at his
sides, his legs splayed out before him. Risa's knees
buckled, then she pulled herself together. Swinging
one pistol back to Trundle, she stumbled to where
Grady rested. Her heart should have been pounding,
but it wasn't doing a thing. Instead, adrenaline and

pure fear keeping her going. Just as she'd done to her dying partner, Risa bent down and jabbed her fingers into Grady's neck.

He opened his eyes.

But as raw relief swamped her, Grady yelled and wrenched his weapon from her, pushing her down to the carpet at the same time. She did a face plant, the rug burning her lower jaw as something whizzed by, inches above her head. She looked up to see Trundle clutching her gun, which he'd laid on the table coming in. He only managed the one shot.

Grady continued to fire until his magazine was empty.

RISA AND GRADY WERE still on the floor when his front door flew open. Four men in black with a battering ram charged inside, then three men with automatic weapons followed as instructed, Grady and Risa threw up their hands and stayed where they were.

Four of the SWAT cops dispersed inside the house and checked it room by room while one ran to Trundle, and a second to Risa and Grady. The last man, clearly the team leader, stood by the front door. The officer checking Trundle looked up and shook his head once, then the other four returned with an "All clear." The leader walked to where Grady and Risa sat.

"We checked through the windows with a camera," he said almost apologetically, "but we had to make sure it was safe." He threw a look over his shoulder. "Get your kit, Riley, and check these officers for injuries. Barnes, call for a wagon. Lee, give Communications a heads up."

Grady watched the team follow orders as quickly and efficiently as he and Risa had when they'd heard, "Hands up." As the officer continued to organize things, however, Grady let his head slump to the chair at his back, the last of his adrenaline seeping away, weary disbelief replacing it. His eyes met Risa's. "Are you okay?"

"I'm okay," she said. "But how did you know to come back inside? I was so afraid you were going to come through the front door. That was his plan. He was going to shoot you then."

Grady explained the burglar alarm and camera then winced as the medical officer began to clean his wound.

"I know it hurts." The SWAT cop looked at Grady with sympathy in her eyes. "But it's a superficial wound. I don't think you even need stitches. You're gonna have a whopper of a headache tomorrow, though." She smoothed a bandage onto his temple then stood and motioned to Risa. "Let me take a look at you now."

When the woman finished and declared her fine,

Risa thanked her and returned to Grady. She blinked several times before she could speak. "You risked your life coming back in here like that. I…"

He raised his hand, and even though it was blood-stained, he laid a finger across her lips. "I did the same thing you would have done in my place."

Her voice was serious, but a light shone in her eyes he'd never seen before. "You'd make someone a damn good partner. How come I never knew what a good shooter you are?"

He shook his head then groaned at the movement. "It wasn't important until now."

"What other skills are you hiding?"

"Too many to name and a few you don't even want to know about."

She cradled his jaw in her hand, then leaned over and gently kissed him. "I want to know about all of them," she said quietly. "There aren't going to be any more secrets between the two of us. It's my turn to investigate you—and I'm gonna take the rest of my life to do it."

SUNSHINE POURED through the window and coated the breakfast table with light. At Grady's end, the place mats were covered with a pile of books and notepads. Concentrating to the exclusion of everything else, he was bent over a journal with a yellow Hi-Liter clutched in his hand.

At Risa's end, a single cup of coffee cooled, a squiggle of steam rising above it. She rustled the newsletter she held, folded it then laid it down with a sigh.

Grady looked up. No more able to resist her now, six months later, than he'd been able to the day they'd met, he stood and came to her side. Crouching down so he could look into her eyes, he put his arms around her, then leaned over and kissed her. "What's wrong?"

"I hate that you're always right."

He shrugged and pursed his lips. "I'm sorry, sweetheart. I know it's a terrible fault, but I can't seem to help myself." Nuzzling her neck, he kissed her again, then leaned back. "What did I do this time?"

She tapped the paper. "Page four. *HPD News.* Have you read it?"

He opened his eyes in mock surprise. "Have I read it? Why on earth would I want to read that rag? I'm a member of the professorial elite, now." He raised his voice and spoke in singsong. "I'm a college pro-fess-or. I don't have to keep up with the pedestrian goings-on at HPD."

"Still, you might want to check out the article." She looked out the window then back at him. "You predicted it would be there."

Puzzled, Grady flipped to the page she'd indicated

and skimmed the headlines until he came to the one she'd obviously meant.

Veteran Officer Cleared In Shooting.

The article gave very few details but emphatically stated that Risa had been exonerated. Had the full extent of Kurt Trundle's actions been revealed, no one would have believed them anyway. Grady hadn't, especially when the crime lab had called him after they'd repeated the ballistics tests.

Kurt Trundle had stolen Risa's gun from the club the night she'd left it to have the trigger adjusted. Not wanting to advertise their incompetence, the range hadn't reported the incident, but when the owner had been questioned, he'd admitted what had happened, including the bizarre fact that an eviscerated dog had been found in a Dumpster two doors down. Trundle had shot the animal then dug out the flattened bullet. He'd forced Lawton Calvin into substituting that slug for the one the coroner had removed from Luke Rowling's body. Since the slug was identical in shape and size to the other slugs recovered from Risa's gun—and even damaged as if it had hit a man—nothing had differentiated the recovered slugs. In case anyone questioned the coroner, Trundle had even made sure to use the same diameter ammunition. Rowling's entrance wound had matched the size of Risa's round as well.

At the end of the article, Melinda Rowling got a

single-sentence mention. The widow of the slain officer, it read, had moved back to Alabama to be near relatives. Leaving the poor woman with a shred of dignity, the report left out what only Grady knew. Those same relatives would be taking care of Melinda's son while she checked into a nearby mental hospital.

When he finished reading, Grady raised his eyes to Risa's. Her gaze held pain but determination, too. Even though the facts had been revealed, as he'd known would be the case, Risa had not been welcomed back into the fold with open arms. In fact, some of her friends still seemed distant. This skimpy article would do nothing to help that situation.

He brushed her cheek with the back of his finger, his heart swelling with tenderness over her obvious distress. "You didn't expect anything more, did you?"

"Not really. But it would have been nice to see it on page one at the very least."

"Everyone who cares knows the real story."

She nodded.

"It doesn't matter." Standing up, he pulled her into his arms and held her tightly. "You were completely cleared. We have a great life ahead of us. We love each other. What more do you need?"

She tightened her arms around his neck. "I want my old life back."

"Do you really?" He smoothed her hair. "I wasn't in your old life."

"You know what I mean," she said. "I want to be an ordinary cop with a job that I do every day, the way I'm supposed to. I don't want to be the one they point to behind my back and go 'she's the one they thought shot her partner.'"

"You can't be anyone other than who you are." He rubbed her shoulders. "But if I were you, I'd stop worrying about my reputation. Your father carries a lot of weight at HPD and he's telling everyone who'll listen how great a cop you are."

She made a face, but behind the dismissive expression, Grady knew a different set of emotions lingered. After things had settled down, Ed Taylor had called Grady to check on Risa and his gravelly voice had been a perfect match to the one Grady had heard on his cell phone the night he'd gotten the tip about Melinda. Taylor's information might have been wrong, but his heart was in the right place. Later on, Grady had told Risa about everything her father had done to try to help her. Her attitude had softened slightly after that and they'd even gotten together with the old man once or twice. Ed Taylor might not ever be able to make things okay with his daughter, but Grady had to give him credit. He was trying his best.

"Your brothers are defending you, too."

She shook her head. "I needed their support six months ago."

"You needed a lot of things six months ago," Grady answered. "But fortunately for us, every day's a new day, and that's all that matters. You keep doing your job and do it well. Pretty soon, they'll forget. Another scandal will come along and yours will be history."

"What about my friends? Are they history, too?"

Grady loved Risa with a fierceness that continued to surprise him, but his eyes were wide-open, too. Late one night after they'd made love, Risa had acknowledged she would probably have reacted the same as her friends had the situation been reversed.

"It was inevitable, I guess," she said. "The relationship the five of us had wasn't sustainable as it was—people change and friendships turn into something else or even disappear entirely. I had to protect myself and I paid the price for that."

Despite her words, Grady knew she still carried the pain of their rejections.

Grady dropped his arms from Risa's shoulders and reached into his pocket. Pulling out a money clip, he peeled off a dollar bill. "Hold out your hand."

She held out her palm and he placed the bill on it, closing her fingers with his own. "I'm not a betting man, so this doesn't constitute a wager." He paused. "But why don't you put this somewhere safe and we'll revisit the argument after things have cooled down. Your friends are still your friends and they always were. *You* stepped back from them as far as *they* stepped back from you. When the time is right, you'll all come together again. Just like you and your dad will."

She looked skeptical, but she tucked the dollar into her pocket. When her eyes came back to his, they were glistening as she wrapped her arms around his neck. "How'd you get to be so smart?" she asked huskily.

"I wasn't that way until I met you," he teased. "You stimulate me…into thinking harder."

She grinned. "Well, I don't have to be at work until seven tonight and your class doesn't start until six. That means we've got all day. How about us doing some…thinking…together?"

He bent his head and kissed her, his lips giving her the answer she wanted to hear. "I love you, Risa," he murmured a moment later. "How I love you."

"I love you, too, Grady." Her tears welled up and spilled down her cheeks. She made no attempt to wipe them off. "Thank you for believing in me."

He kissed her again, then pulled back to look at her. "I always did," he said. "And I always will. That's what love's all about. We're partners now… for life."

Turn the page for an excerpt from the
second book in the
WOMEN IN BLUE *series.*
Sherry Lewis's
THE CHILDREN'S COP
is available from
Harlequin Superromance books
in November 2004.

CHAPTER ONE

LEAVES RUSTLED in the wind and moonlight spilled across the lawn as Lucy Montalvo locked her car and started up the sidewalk toward her Houston condo. Every muscle in her body was sore, and the dull headache that had been teasing her all afternoon had spread across her forehead and settled behind one eye.

A few porch lamps still burned away the late-night shadows and the soft blue flicker of a TV lit a couple of nearby windows, but most of the complex was dark. Usually, Lucy battled a slight loneliness when she came home after her neighbors were asleep, but tonight was different.

She walked slowly, trying to find solace in the near-silence, the autumn breeze that stirred the heavy humid air and the faint glimmer of starlight overhead. The temperature had dropped from its midday high, but the humidity had been unbearable all day and the Texas heat still lingered close to the ground.

Lucy had no idea how late it was. She'd lost track

of time while holding Maria Avila's hand, trying to offer comfort. She wanted to wipe away the memory of little Tomas Avila's body, discovered by a couple of construction workers earlier that afternoon, but it was a scene she knew she'd never forget. She was just grateful that she'd been able to keep his grieving mother from the sight.

Days like this left her feeling slow and lethargic. Lucy was more than ready for some time off, but she wasn't going to let anything get in the way of bringing Tomas's killer to justice.

Much as Lucy loved her career, the constant search for missing children sometimes got to her. Six years after graduating from the Police Academy and hiring on with the Houston Police Department, she still hadn't learned how to lock her heart away. Even her training as a patrol officer and the years she'd spent in the Domestic Violence Unit hadn't hardened her.

A few months ago, she could have released some of tonight's tension and despair over margaritas with the six-pack, a group of friends she'd made during her training in the Academy. For the grueling six months the course lasted, Risa Taylor, Crista Santiago, Abby Carlson and Mei Lu Ling had been as close to Lucy as sisters. Together with Catherine Tanner, their favorite instructor, they'd formed a bond they'd all believed would never break. After their training ended, they'd remained close friends, getting together at least once a month for lunch, more often when their schedules allowed.

The six-pack would have understood both the grim reality of finding Tomas Avila too late, and the pain of having to carry that news to his mother. Abby and Risa would have known the right things to say. Catherine, now chief of police, would have offered advice tempered with experience and wisdom. Mei Lu and Crista would have done their best to chase away the gloom.

But Lucy had helped to break their bond a few months earlier when Risa had been suspected of shooting her partner. Though Risa had been cleared, the friendship had been a casualty, and the other members of the six-pack were the last people Lucy could turn to now.

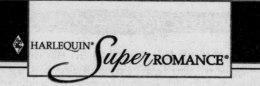

HARLEQUIN *Super*ROMANCE®

YOU, ME & THE KIDS

Caleb's Christmas Wish
by Debra Salonen

Dear Santa: I need a new mommy and daddy. God took mine to Heaven, and they can't come back. Ally and Jake are taking care of me now, and I need them to stay forever. That's all I want for Christmas. Thank you. Caleb.

Allison Jeffries would give anything to make her four-year-old godson's Christmas happier. But she can't be his mother, and from everything she's heard, Jake Westin, Caleb's godfather, won't be his father.

**Available November 2004 wherever
Harlequin Superromance books are sold**

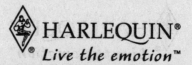

HARLEQUIN®
Live the emotion™

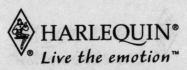

Christmas comes to

HARLEQUIN ROMANCE®

In November 2004, don't miss:

CHRISTMAS EVE MARRIAGE
(#3820)

by Jessica Hart

In this seasonal romance, the only thing Thea is looking for on her long-awaited holiday is a little R and R—she certainly doesn't expect to find herself roped into being Rhys Kingsford's pretend fiancée!

A SURPRISE CHRISTMAS PROPOSAL
(#3821)

by Liz Fielding

A much-needed job brings sassy Sophie Harrington up close and personal with rugged bachelor Gabriel York in this festive story. But how long before he realizes that Sophie isn't just for Christmas—but for life…?

Available wherever Harlequin books are sold.

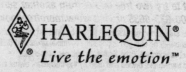

HARLEQUIN®
Live the emotion™

www.eHarlequin.com

HRCTJHLF

If you enjoyed what you just read,
then we've got an offer you can't resist!

Take 2 bestselling
love stories FREE!
Plus get a FREE surprise gift!

Clip this page and mail it to Harlequin Reader Service®

IN U.S.A.	IN CANADA
3010 Walden Ave.	P.O. Box 609
P.O. Box 1867	Fort Erie, Ontario
Buffalo, N.Y. 14240-1867	L2A 5X3

YES! Please send me 2 free Harlequin Superromance® novels and my free surprise gift. After receiving them, if I don't wish to receive anymore, I can return the shipping statement marked cancel. If I don't cancel, I will receive 6 brand-new novels every month, before they're available in stores. In the U.S.A., bill me at the bargain price of $4.69 plus 25¢ shipping and handling per book and applicable sales tax, if any*. In Canada, bill me at the bargain price of $5.24 plus 25¢ shipping and handling per book and applicable taxes**. That's the complete price, and a savings of at least 10% off the cover prices—what a great deal! I understand that accepting the 2 free books and gift places me under no obligation ever to buy any books. I can always return a shipment and cancel at any time. Even if I never buy another book from Harlequin, the 2 free books and gift are mine to keep forever.

135 HDN DZ7W
336 HDN DZ7X

Name	(PLEASE PRINT)	
Address	Apt.#	
City	State/Prov.	Zip/Postal Code

Not valid to current Harlequin Superromance® subscribers.

Want to try two free books from another series?
Call 1-800-873-8635 or visit www.morefreebooks.com.

* Terms and prices subject to change without notice. Sales tax applicable in N.Y.
** Canadian residents will be charged applicable provincial taxes and GST.
   All orders subject to approval. Offer limited to one per household.
   ® are registered trademarks owned and used by the trademark owner and or its licensee.

SUP04R   ©2004 Harlequin Enterprises Limited

A Family Christmas
by Carrie Alexander

(Harlequin Superromance #1239)

All Rose Robbin ever wanted was a family
Christmas—just like the ones she'd seen on TV—but
being a Robbin (one of those Robbins) pretty much
guaranteed she'd never get one. Especially after
circumstances had her living "down" to
everyone else's expectations.

After a long absence, Rose is back in Alouette,
primarily to help out her impossible-to-please mother,
but also to keep tabs on the child she wasn't allowed
to keep. Working hard, helping her mother and trying
to steal glimpses of her child seem to be all that's in
Wild Rose's future—until the day single father
Evan Grant catches her in the act.

NORTH COUNTRY
Stories

Alouette, Michigan.
Located high on the Upper
Peninsula—home to strong
men, stalwart women and
lots and lots of trees.

Available in November 2004 *wherever Harlequin books are sold*

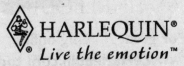

HARLEQUIN®
Live the emotion™

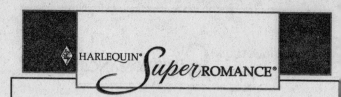
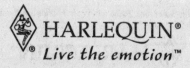